Sarah Sawyer
# A Call To Justice

# Sarah Sawyer
# A Call To Justice

## By: S.W. Andersen

swandersenwrites.com

# ACKNOWLEDGEMENT

Book three has been a labor of love for a series and cast of characters I hold dear to my heart. This one took a while to come together, and I send my deepest gratitude to my friends and beta readers who provided feedback in helping craft the story, as I had been stuck more times than not. While this is a work of historical fiction, the storyline, sadly, continues to play out in 2021.

This idea was born from a desire to shift the focus of the characters to events of the time. Having spent a week on the Crow Indian reservation in 2010, I felt the need to tell the story of the Native Americans. I had the chance to see the pride they have in their culture despite the hardships they still suffer daily. They are strong and proud, and during my research, I learned so much more about the courage and plight of the American Indian.

To this very day, their mistreatment continues. People think of grand casinos and wealth when they think of tribes, but that couldn't be farther from the truth. Poverty rates in the Crow reservation alone this year are at 25%, double the national average. Poor health, addiction, inadequate schools, limited resources including lack of internet, language barriers are just a few of the battles they face. In addition, a growing number of Native American and Indigenous women are being murdered and abducted across states such as Montana without any justice. Their family's concerns dismissed by authorities. Their needs an afterthought by all.

Adding to the insult, they are continually underrepresented. Many national databases list them as "other," affecting their chances at political seats, funding, and more. This lack of representation has never been more apparent than this year's pandemic and how it has hindered their ability to get aid.

Even now, with all the land that's been stolen over the years, the government continually reaches for more in the name of progress. But still, Native Americans hang onto their culture and work to get ahead. They strive every day to make life better for the next generation—to go to college, get better jobs, provide programs for youth, and to improve health. The true natives to our land don't ask for handouts, only for recognition and the return of what was rightfully theirs. I hope this can help shed some light on their story. Portions of the proceeds from the sale of this book will go to programs benefiting college scholarships and ending violence against indigenous women.

The National Indigenous Women's Resource Center

https://www.niwrc.org/donate.

American Indian College Fund

standwithnativestudents.org/

I'd like to send a big thank you to the due diligence and dedication of Linda North, who contributed tremendous time and effort to the fine tuning of this book and helped me grow as a writer.

A huge shout out to my very talented friend, Cindy Bamford, for once again delivering a fantastic cover that captures the essence of this series.

A tip of the cowboy hat to Lee Winter for working up an action packed blurb in minutes, where I had bumbled for hours. As always, I am in awe of your talent.

Of course, deep love and appreciation goes to my wife, Dianna, for her patience and understanding while putting up with the many days I spent locked inside my head conjuring up another Sarah Sawyer adventure.

And to all of you, the readers, I am continually grateful for your support and inspiration. Thank you!

# DEDICATION

There is nothing like the love of a mother, or the love of a horse.

For my mom, Carol, my cowgirl hero, and for the five gentle giants who have blessed me with their love and friendship over the years: Silver, Jet, Dodie, Ebony, Brandy, and Rebel. Thank you for the adventures and the life lessons.

# CHAPTER ONE

**Two Years Later-Ketchum, Idaho**

*Sarah*

For years I had walked in the valley of the shadow of death, fearing nothing, feeling nothing—not wanting to die, but not giving much thought to a life ahead. Not until the very blood that had led me there also led me back into the light. Twice. Now, as I stared out the window at all we'd built, I was surrounded by life. The crops we'd grown. The livestock we'd raised. The family we'd forged. The love we'd cultivated. On the rare occasion when I'd taken a step back to look at how far I'd come, there'd been a sense of awe. And I owed it all to Jo, the woman whose depth of love and strength of patience bested my stubbornness.

Stretching my limbs, I sucked in a deep breath of warm summer air and tried to ignore the stiffness that reminded me I was getting older. Hard to believe only a few years ago, the majority of my nights were spent on the hard grounds I'd traveled, though the nagging aches served as a daily reminder. When a familiar warm body engulfed me from behind, all soreness vanished. Jo's soft lips graced my neck, and I seriously considered leaving my chores for another day. Other needs required tending to. Important ones.

"Good morning," she said, her breath tickling my ear. The low hum of her voice against my back did things to me that defied explanation.

"It is now." I pulled her left hand up to my lips and greeted them with a kiss.

"There you go with that sweet talk again. You know where that'll get ya."

"I do." A smile rolled up, waiting for her to challenge my work ethic. I didn't have to wait long. Jo slipped around in front with one of those teasing grins upon her lips, the very definition of temptation in the flesh.

"Whatever happened to my hardworking cowgirl?" Her long dark hair had been pulled up, but a few incorrigible tendrils fell to her collarbone.

"Oh, I promise I'll be working hard."

Brushing the hair back over her shoulder, I licked my lips, ready to taste her skin. Jo's head lulled back as a deep laugh escaped, teasing me with her slender neck that called to my mouth the way a whistle beckoned a horse. My gaze traveled lower, and my heart kicked up into a gallop at the sight of her. Jo stood before me in nothing but my blue shirt parted open down the center, barely covering her breasts. Long legs descended from the hem.

So beautiful.

"And it'll be extremely rewarding," I added, a low growl rumbling out.

Seeing Jo in my clothes drove me wild. She didn't do it often, but when she did, breath became a rarity. I slipped my hands under the shirt and curled my callous-hardened fingers into her soft flesh. Jo's smile agreed with my suggestion. I leaned in and nudged her softly with my nose before capturing her lips in a kiss—tender and slow at first.

Jo was to be savored until I could resist the urge to devour her no longer. My hands drifted lower, taking time to caress her curves on their journey to their favorite place at the swell of her ass. Firm pressure brought her body flush to mine, instigating a gasp from us both. The fuse had been lit. Tenderness gave way to feverishness as her tongue met mine.

Jo's fingers worked to undo the buttons of my shirt as I walked her backward toward our bedroom. Our lips barely parted for more than a breath. Sliding the shirt off Jo's shoulders, I couldn't wait to feel her bare beneath me. Her knees hit the bed, and she fell back, legs slightly parted, chest flushed a lovely pink all the way to her cheeks, a come-hither grin stretching to her eyes. No more lovely sight existed than Jo spread out for me and nothing on this earth felt better than being skin to skin with her.

My hands, fast enough to kill the most skilled gunfighter, failed to move at an acceptable speed to free me of my clothes. As I fumbled with my belt, a low rumble of hoofbeats outside brought my movements to a painful halt.

"Dammit," I muttered between heavy breaths. The struggle to settle myself was nearly impossible with Jo still laying there ready, and unfortunately, waiting.

"I have stronger words," Jo rasped out, breathless and frustrated. Her head dropped back against the bed, and her arms fell limp at her sides in defeat. After a humorless laugh, she propped back up on her elbows and stared at me. Her bottom lip slid between her teeth and darkened hazel eyes screamed out the very same demands as my body.

"I love you," I said, feeling the truth of it screaming in every inch of my body as I stepped back. A bone-deep ache of regret stiffened my fingers as I buttoned up my shirt and stared down at her with a hunger that burned my insides. The fiery need would remain unfulfilled.

"I love you too. Be careful out there." Jo sat up to adjust my collar. Her fingertips ghosted across my skin, sending a pleasurable shiver throughout my body. She cupped my cheek and gave me a knowing smile. Why she enjoyed teasing me, I might never know, but I'd never ask her to stop. After stealing one last kiss, I mustered the strength to leave. I walked outside with a glare that made my displeasure widely apparent.

"You're early, Jessie."

"I'd apologize, but you know I wouldn't mean it." Steely gray eyes narrowed in jest from under her dusty white hat. Long brown hair fell over her shoulders, framing her face reddened by long days under the summer heat. Her gun sat low on her hip and Silver, her green broke dapple-gray gelding, refused to sit still.

"Hmph." Making a show of stomping out to the barn did little to relieve the coil of tension low in my belly.

Jessie let out a sharp huff as she trailed behind. "Somebody's frustrated. If I'm gonna have to deal with this all day, maybe I should let you finish what you started."

"The moment's passed, thank you very much, so you can suffer the consequences."

"How have we managed to stay friends?" Her usual sarcasm laced her words before ending with a laugh.

That damned cocky smirk begged to be wiped from her face. Though the thought had crossed my mind numerous times over the years, I had only acted upon the urge once. That had been one heck of a fight.

"I have no idea." I shrugged my shoulders and chuckled. "You can be one aggravating horse's ass."

"Me? You can be downright insufferable."

"Don't use them big words with me, Marshal."

We stared one another down. The corners of Jessie's mouth curled up as long and slow as mine until we both barked out a laugh. Clover whinnied with excitement as I slipped the bridle over her head and led her out.

"What's got you two in fits?" Jo appeared dressed in riding breeches and my blue shirt with the top two buttons undone, arms crossed, and a challenging brow arched. We quieted down quick as kids caught with a handful of Mama's cookies. An amused grin claimed Jo's lips as she shook her head. "Two peas in a pod, you are. Both annoyingly stubborn as mules, but good of heart."

Long, graceful strides carried her to me, glancing up to offer Jessie a good morning as she passed. "I'll feed up so you can get goin'." She kissed me on the cheek and whispered in my ear, "Maybe we can finish what we started later...if you're not too tired."

I cleared my throat and forced my eyes away from the temptation of soft skin she'd left in clear view. Clover stomped her hoof into the dirt, anxious to get to work. I dug deep for the strength to step away from Jo, who looked far too proud of herself. She grinned at me and stroked Clover's neck as I saddled up.

"Looks like it'll be an early day," Jessie commented, looking irritatingly smug.

"Shut it, Jessie," I grumbled like a child.

Jo laughed and kissed me again.

"How's the head count?" I asked as the sheep settled into their new pasture.

The herd immediately began devouring the long blades of grass. The lack of rain had made it necessary to move pastures every couple of weeks to protect the grass we did have. The shift to wool sheep over the last few years had been a learning process, but a profitable one. We still raised some cattle, but sheep and farming had become our focus.

"They're all here." Jessie wiped the sweat from her hands, then recorded the number in her book. She closed it, then stuffed it into her saddlebag.

"Good." I slid gently from the saddle and stretched my stiff limbs. "Been hearin' rumblin's of missin' head 'round town."

"Maybe we should do some night watches."

"Probably." Removing my hat to wipe the sweat and dust from my brows, I looked to the sky and groaned at the endless miles of clear blue. The sun sat up high in the sky, causing the scattered bits of snow upon the mountain peaks to glisten. It would have been a picture perfect day if it hadn't been for the ungodly heat and drought. "It's one helluva hot summer. Sure would be nice to get some rain."

"Sure would be nice to get some whiskey," Jessie countered.

"That's always nice." A laugh tickled my words. I set my hat back on my head. "But for now, I'll settle for a shade tree and this here canteen." Holding up my old can, I nodded toward the towering cluster of trees.

"Brought lunch too," I added, reaching into my worn out saddlebags. Their leather had thinned at the bottom, on the edge of wearing through. Those old, second-hand bags had been there for the lows and the highs of my life like a best friend.

Shuffling through the random contents of rope, nails, rags, and tools, my fingers finally latched onto the bag of jerky I'd made. I pulled it out and held it up like a prized catch.

Jessie's stomach growled. "Perfect. I'm starvin'. I got some cherries, but they won't fill you up much."

"They'll be good in the heat though."

After giving Clover her fill at the small pond, I started the hundred-yard trek toward cooler temps on foot while Clover kept pace at my side. She was getting older but showed no signs of slowing down. My girl still loved the trails, loved to work, and she loved me as much as I did her.

"Having fun, girl?"

Clover grunted and gave me a loving nudge with her muzzle.

"Yeah, me too. And I'm glad you're enjoying those green pastures."

A whinny was her response, her head bouncing up and down in agreement.

"You two talkin' bout me?" Jessie trotted up alongside. Her lips quirked into a teasing smile.

"Always. Right girl?"

Again, Clover whinnied and nodded.

"I knew it. I can't imagine all the lies you fill her head with."

My laugh fell to a sigh of relief when we were finally gifted with the shade created by thick branches covered with lush green leaves. The only sounds were the whisper of wind across their edges and our steady breaths. I let Clover graze, and I sank against the base of the tree. Long gulps of water soothed my parched throat. The trails of spillover were equally appreciated, cooling my skin as the breeze danced over me.

Once Jessie's horse found his own place to indulge, Jessie dropped like a heap beside me. She pulled out her canteen and took huge gulps that ended in a sigh of relief. The two of us sat there staring at the herd and sharing our food.

Long silences were one of the things I enjoyed most about Jessie. After all these years, we were comfortable with quiet between us. She'd always been a woman of few words, and I'd always been content with the sounds of nature and the ramblings of my own thoughts—the makings of a perfect friendship. Jackie also respected our preferences, something I appreciated as much as her loyalty.

Jo did too, mostly, except for when she was being Jo—meaning hell-bent on getting an answer out of me. And Jade, bless her heart, could barely go thirty seconds without making a sound—just one of the reasons I had suggested she stick with Jo whenever Nick came to help out at the farm. She made the livestock jumpy, buzzing around like a bee all the time. Our family had its quirks, but we all had one another's backs. What more could a person ask for?

"Hey, Sarah?"

"Yeah?"

"Did you ever dream you'd have all this?"

At first, I laughed at the question and replied, "I mostly had nightmares." However, a pause of reflection brought me to a sad conclusion. "Honestly though, I didn't think I'd live." I tipped my head enough to see the veil of sympathy fall over her expression, but I refused to meet her eyes. "I mean, I hoped, but…"

"Yeah." A somber nod and another moment of silence stretched before she spoke again. "And then you met Jo."

"And then I met Jo." Jo—beautiful, strong, and oh so unexpected—had definitely changed everything. The simple thought of her brightened me from the inside out, so much so that even Jessie smiled. "Only took one night with Jo, and I looked for any reason to get back to her. The only times I did dare to dream, it was of settlin' down in a little house with her. But to have all this? What we've all built together as a family? To even have a family again? Not even in my wildest dreams."

Jessie nodded. She took another slug of water from her canteen and wiped her chin with the back of her hand.

"It's nice the dream came true, more than I ever could've imagined, but I still have nightmares," I reluctantly admitted. "Only now, they're about losin' it all."

"I have 'em too, but we'll face whatever comes, together, like always. And we will win."

I nodded, feeling the strength in her support, but gathered no relief from my deepest fear. No matter how good things were, I still envisioned the worst lingering on the horizon. Probably because I'd usually been right. With any luck, one of these days I'd be proven wrong.

"What about you?" I asked, shutting the door on my cycle of thoughts. "Did you dream of this?"

"Definitely." A short burst of laughter bubbled out. "You know I grew up on a small farm, and deep down, I always wanted that again. After all those years travelin' though, I wondered if I could actually settle down. There was such freedom in havin' no attachment."

"Believe me, I understand."

For a time, I had longed for a return to the trails, no matter how brief, but it had been a long while since I'd given it much thought. I had slowly managed to set down roots and embrace them. The realization struck me with a mix of sadness and relief that plunged me into the depths of my own mind until another chuckle rumbling out of my old friend shook me from my thoughts.

"I like it more than I thought I would, bein' a homebody," she said. Her smile grew, then faded like the evening sun. "I miss Jackie when I'm gone. Those trips takin' the herd to market, all I want to do is get home to her." Jessie's lips pulled into a thin line as the longing in her words hovered around us.

"One of these days you'll be too old to ride out. Then you can sit on the porch, whine about how you miss it, and complain about the weather," I offered, hoping for a return of her smile.

Jessie and I were a rare breed of woman. Our journeys had not been easy, but we survived, and it was nice to hear she had found a home. She'd always insisted I deserved to be happy, but I felt she deserved happiness more. Now, it was hers.

"This kinda talk sounds like we're already old." Jessie laughed and slapped me on the shoulder.

"Maybe, but that's a badge I'd wear, and with honor."

"Me too, old friend. Me too."

"And, Jessie, if you don't want to move the herd anymore, I can get George. Or hire on another."

"Thanks. I'm not ready to quit yet, but I'll keep that in mind."

"Shall we get back home then?"

"I know some ladies that would be happy if we did."

We both struggled to get to our feet, groaning like the two old ladies we were on the road to becoming. Despite sharing a laugh over our aches and pains, Jessie wore an unrecognizable expression that set me on the edge of worry. She had something on her mind today, but I wouldn't rush her to explain. She'd reveal all in her own time.

"I'm happy for you, ya know? For all of us. We've been through so much," she said soon after. I thanked the heavens I didn't have to wait days or weeks for her to let go. Jessie tipped her hat back and looked at me as she continued, "But mostly for you—that you found someone who could give you back what you lost. I hope you know that."

Those gray eyes held mine for a long, meaningful moment.

"I do. And thank you."

The confession seemed to hold a particular importance to her I couldn't quite grasp. How long had she been holding that in? Was it because of our intimate history? Did she think I believed otherwise? Worse yet, did she think I didn't wish her the same good fortunes? We may have had some rough spots, but I would leave no question of the sort for anyone as important to me as Jessie.

"I'm happy for you too," I said, keeping a hold of her gaze. A gentle squeeze of my hand on her shoulder hoped to reinforce my sincerity. Since neither of us were fond of airing our emotions out in the open, I lightened the mood. "Whatever you're drinkin' today, you should have it more often. Makes havin' you around much more palatable." I tossed her a wink and gave her a slap on the back.

She relaxed and allowed a grin to return once again. "Pfft. You think you're so funny. Horse's ass."

"As I recall, you love my ass. None finer in seven states, you said." Ah, reminiscing could be such fun.

Jessie cringed, not sharing my enthusiasm. "Let's never tell Jo that," she muttered as she grabbed her horse's reins. "Or Jackie."

"Agreed."

Sharing a smile, we mounted up and headed for home. There was no sweeter word in my world.

# CHAPTER TWO

"INDIANS KILL FAMILY OF FOUR."

The headline in big bold print dominated the front page of the paper. Seemed everything this side of the Mississippi was in turmoil as more people headed west. A quick glance through the facts and the story appeared to match the theme of the last few weeks. Travelers caught and killed by the murdering "savages."

That description didn't match any of the Indians I had ever encountered. Indians didn't search out a fight. But maybe they'd grown tired of the mistreatment and wanted revenge? I certainly couldn't pass any judgement there. I could understand their pain and anger at the way they'd been treated. Our government had been disgustingly brutal, and even with a treaty signed, they found ways to run them off their own lands in the name of bettering the country.

Fortunately, our town had kept its peace. Carter had worked hard to keep it that way. I rolled the paper up and stuffed it under my arm to read after dinner. When Jo came out of the store, we started toward the sheriff's office. Jo kept in step with me as we crossed the busy street. Seemed everyone had decided to get an early start today, the brutal summer heat playing a part in their planning.

"Mornin', Sarah. Mornin', Jo."

"Mornin', Mr. Kines. Mrs. Kines," we replied in unison as the old couple passed.

I tipped my hat, full eye contact with them both, standing tall and proud. Gone were the days of downcast eyes and peering up from under the safety of my wide brim. Gone too, were the whispers, cautious glances, the scurrying away whenever I'd approach. Boy, I sure missed those days whenever a foul mood struck. Still ever present, however, were the occasional heated, roaming gazes from female passersby. Though I'd like to say their flirtations had no effect on me, like anyone else, ego puffed its chest at having drawn their attention. Like the new girl at the general store, Rose—eyes only for me, smile tugging at her lips as she grew closer.

"Good morning, Sarah." Her words rolled out low and sensuous.

"Mornin', Rose," I greeted the same as anyone else, giving no sign of interest. I truly had none other than the sense of flattery, and I ignored the lingering of her eyes as she crossed my path closer than necessary.

A clearing of throat drew my attention to Jo on my right, one accusing brow arched high, something between a smirk and a glower on her face. Her eyes held a sense of scolding. Feverish heat raced up my neck to my face. I coughed and looked away.

"What?" I asked, hopefully hiding the guilty feeling, though I'd done nothing wrong.

An annoyed huff blew out and her lip curled. "You know what."

Adjusting my hat and clearing my throat, I said, "You have nothing to worry about."

"Oh, I know," she said, more than confident. "But I may need to make it clear to someone else."

A laugh bellowed out. "I don't think that will be necessary," I said, though her possessiveness filled me with more warmth than any heated gaze.

"Let's hope not." Despite her words, she adjusted her posture, settling her shoulders back to appear taller, more imposing. The hem of her scarlet dress glided an inch above the dirt as she moved with the grace of royalty.

I offered my elbow for Jo to latch on. Her subtle smirk came as a sign of approval. We rarely engaged in such behavior in public, but it felt needed. Her arm fit snug in the crook of my elbow as we continued on our way. Our town had added half a dozen more buildings over the last couple of years, stretching its length now to nearly a mile long.

Jo leaned in. "You enjoyed it though, didn't you?"

Of course she wouldn't let it lie. I knew better than to deny, but I also knew something else. "Same as you do when Annemarie does it."

Her mouth floundered open and closed like a river trout gasping for air. "It is a nice compliment, I suppose," she conceded.

And that was the end of that. Fighting both the urge to say I told you so and the victorious grin straining to make its appearance took the strength of ten horses, but never rub salt unless you wanted it rubbed into you, especially when it came to Jo. She did not take well to taunting.

I knew what she did enjoy though.

"Maybe. But only one woman's smile ever lit me up like a wildfire, and she still sets me aflame every single day."

"You get smoother with age, Sarah Sawyer."

We shared a laugh, but the joy died on the spot when we stepped into Carter's office. The Sheriff looked as pale as a full moon on a clear night. Sunk low into his chair with beads of sweat across his brows, his sunken features appeared more pronounced in the dim light. Jo rushed to his side, but my boots had rooted themselves into the wooden floor.

"Carter, you're burning up," Jo said, her hand pressed to his forehead. She gave him a once over. "You should be at home. Let Ben take over today."

"You're probably right, Jo," he croaked, sounding weak and fragile, so unlike the Carter we knew.

"How'd you slip past Maggie looking like this?" Jo chided in a mothering tone.

"I didn't feel that bad earlier."

"We'd better get you home so you can rest."

Carter struggled to stand as he said, "Let me just find—"

"No." Jo placed her hand on his shoulder, holding Carter in his chair. "I'll find Ben." She looked at me. "Sarah, make sure he gets home, please."

With a nod, I watched as Carter pushed up onto unsteady feet and dragged heavy legs my way. A sickening feeling dropped low in my belly. I couldn't put a finger on the exact emotion, but it resembled that of dread. Our town had done well to avoid the plagues sweeping through the larger cities, but as their people moved west, towns had begun to suffer. Not only from the illnesses they'd brought with them, but the crunch on food and the increase in theft as well. The drought had only made things worse. As I drove the wagon toward Carter's home, the two of us eerily silent, I feared the persistent worries that lingered in the shadows of my happiness were creeping closer.

Leaning on the fence facing the west horizon, I stared at the mountains as the sunset sky ran through its sequence of magnificent colors. Each day a fresh brush taking to canvas, I looked forward to every one of Mother Nature's reveals. Even better, the sight of her artwork painting the sky above the farm we'd built. Pride swelled, lifting my chest, filling me with a heady sense of accomplishment—something I rarely indulged in—and not for the first time, I wondered what my parents would think of my life. How about Mary and Henry? Would they be proud? And what would they think of Jo?

When my thoughts drifted to Carter and Maggie, the feeling deflated. Would they be appreciating the beauty too, or did each setting sun remind them it might be their last together? Was every nightfall a countdown to the end?

In reality, that was the truth for all of us, but when standing on death's door, things took on a different meaning. When you had your hand on the doorknob, looking forward to tomorrow ceased to exist. Memories of once upon a time were celebrated instead. But also true is that sometimes, when you're strong enough, or perhaps lucky enough, you're able to leave the door closed until another day.

I might have had a habit of fearing the worst and believed luck to be a finicky woman, but I had faith the strength within would find ways to persevere. Carter's fate appeared grim. He had looked terrible, and to be honest, he'd been getting thinner the last few weeks. Was the Sheriff a lucky man? I couldn't say, but he was definitely strong.

On second thought, if this was to be the last of his days, Carter could boast of having led a full life, a life to be proud of, and had a loving family. Carter was indeed a lucky man. I could only strive to make my life as fulfilling as his.

Clover trotted up and nudged my arm. I pressed my palm to her white blaze and gave her a rub. Jo slid up behind me, arms wrapping around my waist, locking in front to hold us close. My free hand covered hers. Warm lips met the skin of my neck and they turned upward into a smile, taking my own with them. Both of my girls were here, and their love swept every worry aside.

As much as I still suffered the occasional nightmare of moments passed, I also had a habit of clouding happy moments with worrisome thoughts of the future, but every morning I wake up with Jo in my arms pushes the threatening clouds of doom further away. Though they never leave the horizon, after several quiet years, less time has been spent dwelling on when the next strike of lightning would come. My soul had found happiness, acceptance, and peace—other than thunderstorms, which still made me queasy. I'd never truly get over the horrific memory of losing Jo, but at least such episodes had become few and far between.

Approaching hoofbeats thankfully kept me from dwelling on darkness. We turned to find Jessie and Jackie sharing a saddle on Silver with Jackie's arms wrapped around Jessie's waist, a sunny smile shining bright. The former Marshal sat as tall and stoic as ever as they came to a stop. Happiness radiated from them both.

"Hello, ladies. Anything new goin' on?" Jessie asked.

"Let's see..." I looked skyward, pretending to think. "George and I could use some help shearin' sheep tomorrow." The look on her face had both Jo and I chuckling.

"Damn, maybe I can still get my badge back."

"Oh, no you don't!" Jackie nudged her from behind, still smiling.

"We were just about to enjoy a little fire and a drink, if you'd care to join us," Jo offered.

Jessie and Jackie shared a look of silent questioning before nodding. Jackie swung her leg over and slid down to the ground, followed by Jessie, who walked her horse toward the trough.

Something more lingered behind Jessie's comment, and it rubbed me the wrong way. I excused myself from the others and jogged after her.

"Hey."

"I already know what you're gonna ask," Jessie said flat out without slowing her pace.

"Then...?"

"No, I don't plan to put on another badge." A pause came as she tied off her horse. Her shoulders fell with a heavy exhale of breath. "Of any kind." Jessie turned, and for the first time in my life, I saw fear in them.

"You know, a sheriff got gunned down the other day outside Fort Worth. Not trying to apprehend anyone. Not in a battle. He was just ridin'." Her eyes slid over to Jackie. "Carter's been tryin' to get a few more deputies. I can't say I hadn't been givin' it some thought, but I love her. I couldn't bear to see that look in her eyes again, the one she'd get whenever I used to leave, and well…after hearin' that," she looked back at me, "I choose her. I've done my service."

"You have."

"Yes, I have," she repeated as if to cement the decision.

"It's okay. Let someone else take up the fight."

"You?"

"Oh no. I'm retired too." I slapped her on the back, and we shared an easy laugh, though a brief unsettling twist wrenched my stomach.

"Good." Relief settled into her features as she nodded. "What was it you said to me when I retired? Somethin' about spendin' more time with my girl?"

"Every damned minute you can."

Her eyes crinkled with a wide grin I couldn't remember ever having seen before. "Let's do that then."

As we made our way back to the house, Jackie beamed at Jessie, and Jo's eyes met mine. Boy, how those deep hazels could go right to my heart every damned time. Across the yard and right to her side I went, draping an arm around Jo's waist and placing a kiss to her cheek. Jo sank into my side, her warmth soothing. Jackie and Jessie fell into a similar hold, relaxed and content. We were the picture of a family and moments like this, with all the pieces of my life fitting perfectly together, made me happier than I'd ever imagined being.

Flashes of my parents, of Jo, being ripped away from me struck hard and fast. In crept that fear again, slithering down my spine like a rattlesnake waiting for the moment to strike. For all my strengths, I hadn't been able to slay the demons holding the shroud of darkness over my heart. Fast hands were of no help in the cause, but time, and more nights like these, would help me win the battle.

# CHAPTER THREE

**Jo**

Quiet strength. That was the best way to describe Sarah Sawyer. Sarah possessed something special, something that drew me and everyone else in with few words. A rare find nowadays, she did the hard work without asking for credit. She was who she was—unapologetic, loyal, hardworking, loving, deadly. Her actions spoke volumes, and since Sarah had settled in, she'd become a silent leader in the community. Someone the people leaned on, turned to, trusted. I mentioned it once in passing, and unsurprisingly, Sarah failed to recognize her importance.

I leaned my elbows on the porch rail and watched her work. She sat on the steps repairing saddles, not just her own, but Mr. Jensen's and Doc Smith's as well. The muscles in her forearms flexed as she pulled and twisted the leather into place. Sarah had the mental toughness of the most stubborn of mules, but a couple of years on the ranch had brought visible proof of her physical strength as well. While her hands had hardened and muscles had toned from work, her heart had softened, opening itself unknowingly to an entire town. Once the loner, Sarah Sawyer had found a home, and they embraced her in return.

She glanced up at me, a wry smile on her lips and a glint in her eye. "What?"

"Nothing," I said with a dreamy sigh, resting my chin in my palms. "Just love watching you work with your hands." My words had hit their mark. Beautiful warmth filled her cheeks, turning her skin from tan to deep red.

"Well, you're in luck. I have two more to do tonight." She pulled the next strap through, exaggerating the movement with a teasing smirk.

"I'm glad Mr. Jensen finally gave in and let you fix it. We were afraid it would break and he'd fall off. Not sure he'd fare well at his age."

"Took some doin'. I had to agree to let him help shear the sheep next go round."

I had to laugh at that. Always a negotiation with him. "That's fine. He just wants to feel useful. But I know he appreciates you. Everyone does." The blush struck her cheeks again, and she buried herself further into her work.

"I do what I can. They're good people."

"They are. This town has been lucky. Hope it stays that way."

"We have to be diligent when newcomers settle here. Show them we won't tolerate any other way. Carter's done well keepin' the peace." Her lips pressed into a hard line.

"He has." I looked out over the green fields before gently adding, "I hope the next sheriff will too."

Sarah didn't respond, only stood up to move one saddle aside and slide the next one over before taking her seat again. We'd only ever glanced over the topic. Neither of us wanted Sarah to become sheriff, but there was a tension around us, like fate's invisible thread pulling it towards us in a way that felt inevitable. I'd curse fate if it hadn't been the reason I'd found Sarah. Now, I had to hope it wouldn't take her away.

## Sarah

Three days later, Carter seemed no closer to making a recovery. Who would keep the peace if he no longer could? He'd tried to deputize me before, but I wanted no more part of upholding the law now than I had a couple of years ago. There had been enough bloodshed in my past to last three lifetimes. And besides, I was happy working the ranch. The Doctor had laid down her guns. Someone else could take on the fight.

Perched on my corner stool in the saloon, I looked around the room packed full of patrons. The population had grown, as had the number of businesses. Now we had several places to carry on after a long day, but the core of our once sleepy town remained loyal to Jo and Jade. Hardworking folks who were proud of the place we all called home. That was something I admired about the people I had come to call my family. Loyalty was rare, something I didn't take lightly. Somewhere among them would be a capable sheriff, though hopefully, Carter would be on the mend, and it would become a problem for another day.

Looking for something to take my mind off of such heavy topics, my eyes were drawn to Jo working across the way. A smile began a slow climb up my face, reaching higher when she threw me a wink as she passed. Oh, how I longed to slip around the wooden barrier between us and pull her into a kiss. Maybe I could tempt her into—

*THUNK!*

The suddenness of a pie plunking down in front of me nearly sent me tumbling backward to the floor. Mrs. Jones slid in alongside me, chuckling lightly with deep brown eyes twinkling as she braced me with a gentle press against my back. Those frail old hands were sturdier than they appeared.

"Sorry, Sarah. Didn't mean to sneak up on ya."

A shuddering breath led to an awkward laugh. "It's all right. Guess I was daydreamin'." I focused on the pie in hopes she wouldn't see the heat rushing into my cheeks.

"I'm sure you were." Her tone left no question that my hiding had been in vain. She chuckled again, this time high pitched and giddy before she said, "This is a little something for your help with the fences."

"Looks delicious, but there's no need. That's what friends do for one another."

"And friends also bake pies." Her weathered old hand covered mine. "Please, enjoy."

The aroma of fresh baked cherry goodness could break anyone's resolve. I smiled and looked back up at her. "We will. Thank you."

"That girl," she nodded towards Jo, "has brought nothing but good to this town, including you." Before I could lodge a protest, she powered on,

"It's true. She's helped revitalize this town, starting with this saloon, then her farm. Now, with your help, we all have solid fences, sturdy saddles, and feel safe and secure. Over five hundred people here now, and a bunch more in Hailey. Can you believe it?"

"I appreciate that, though I'm not sure how much safety I provide. Sheriff Carter does well to keep the peace."

"Oh, he does. Carter is a wonderful man, but he's not well."

"I know." My earlier smile fell away.

"You've seen 'em, Sarah. If it's what Fred had, he won't be sheriff much longer, sad to say. And poor Maggie and the kids..."

"He'll be fine. Doc is out there now. He'll help pull Carter through."

Her look of doubt said otherwise. "A badge would look good on ya."

"That's Jessie's job."

"Thought she gave it up?"

"Maybe she'd like a new one. She likes bright, shiny things. And rules."

"All women like bright, shiny things."

I followed her gaze down to my silver revolver with the pearl handle, then sent my attention back to Jo, who gave me a toothy smile as she poured a drink across the way. "Yeah, well, I've found something far brighter I love way more."

"So you have." Mrs. Jones gave Jo a cheeky grin as she approached.

"Can I get you two anything?"

"No thank you, Jo. Just leaving a pie to thank Sarah for all her hard work. She's a keeper."

"I think so." Jo laughed at my uncomfortable shift on the barstool.

"I'll have another whiskey, please," I interjected, hoping to change the topic.

"I must be getting back to Clint. Thank you again." She placed a hand on my shoulder. "Have a nice night, ladies."

"We will. You do the same," Jo replied, then reached for a bottle. She looked at me, grinning as she poured. "I still can't leave you alone for a second. Now you're charmin' the shoes off the little old ladies in town."

"What can I say? They love me."

"They certainly do. I'm jealous." She flashed a playful pout.

"You shouldn't be. I only love you."

Her lips parted, revealing that gorgeous smile. "I know. And I love you."

She slid the glass in front of me, then leaned her elbows on the edge of the bar top, giving me one magnificent view. I licked my lips, unable to distinguish whether my mouth watered from the aroma of the pie or the tempting dessert that was Jo. Either way, she let out a short burst of laughter and shook her head.

"Guess you also love pie," she teased.

"I sure do, but nothin' tastes as good as you, Jo." The corners of her mouth twitched. A flush spread across her chest. Pride swelled at having caused one of those rare moments when I'd been able to leave Jo speechless and blushing.

"One more hour and I'm done," she said, eyes twinkling with mischief. "Gonna wait or head out?"

"I'll wait for ya, but could ya bring me a fork? I can't wait for this pie."

Jo laughed. "Of course, but save me some."

"Maybe," I said, mulling my options. I leaned in closer and whispered, "If you're good."

"Ain't no one better," she whispered back before pressing a kiss to my cheek.

That was the truth.

# CHAPTER FOUR

With a bag in hand, I made sure to wear a smile when I stepped into the sheriff's office. Carter didn't need any more folks with grim expressions around. The office seemed darker than usual and almost unbearably stuffy. No wonder he'd gotten sick. Had it always been that way?

"Hello, Carter. How ya feelin' today?"

Carter was slow to rise, hastily stuffing his handkerchief into his vest pocket as he rose up onto shaky legs. A stain of blood colored the white fabric protruding from his vest, but I didn't let my gaze linger. He wouldn't want the pity. Carter and I were much alike.

"Howdy, Sarah." His words came out low and gravely, punctuated by a cough. A forced but genuine smile graced his lips. "I'm on the mend, thanks to Doc. And Mrs. Chen brought me some tea made from them herbs she grows. Helps a bit."

"Good to hear."

His color had improved but coughing up blood wasn't a good sign. Leaning his weight on the edge of his desk, Carter still held a gleam in his eye. At least he was fighting. I crossed the room and set the bag beside him.

"Brought ya some fresh picked vegetables."

"Appreciate it. Maggie will love it. How's everything out your way?"

"Quiet, thankfully."

"That's good." The pained lines creasing his mouth softened.

"Soil's given us a fair crop, despite the lack of rain, and the livestock's doin' well. We're gonna slaughter one of the cows soon. Need any meat?"

"Count me in. Thank you." His face softened as if the small gesture had somehow taken a load off his shoulders.

"You're welcome." Like every other visit to his office, my attention drifted to the board of wanted postings. The days when my face had hung among them seemed a lifetime ago. I idly wondered if checking them out served as a sort of walk down memory lane. Lately, the postings had mostly been young men, a new wave of thieves and murderers making a name for themselves. "Anything of interest goin' on?"

"Robbery is on the rise. There's a pair makin' news stealin' livestock, but they may have shifted into bank robbin' now."

"How very brave of them."

Carter barked out a laugh. "That new couple, the Marley's, up on the hill? They chased someone out of their barn the other day. I'm happy to say the few deputies we've got have helped keep order, but with more people movin' in during the drought and the silver mines closin', I worry about what might come."

I made a note to tell everyone to keep a sharper eye out around the farms. "I wish they'd stay in the East and leave us alone, but everyone's searchin' for that big dream. If only they knew how hard it was to survive outside those big cities."

"Maybe you could hold sermon and discourage them. If a bunch went back East, it could sway the shift in population. Sarah Sawyer, Savior of the West." He twirled the end of his thick, graying mustache as he wheezed a little laugh in delight.

"What a title that would be." A light chuckle rumbled my chest at the thought. "But they won't listen."

"Afraid your right." He shook his head. "I doubt I could live in New York, not that I've ever been. Just from what I read and heard."

"I've been there."

"Well now, that's a surprise." He settled more of his weight atop his desk, weariness taking over his posture but intrigue brightening his expression.

"I took a chance once," I said, shrugging off the magnitude of the move with indifference. "Hoped to start a new life and forget." Sometimes it felt like yesterday, a young girl with no thought of her future, running from the horrors of her past. Most days though, it was near impossible to remember a time in my adult life when I wasn't this version of me—with a gun on my hip and a clear intent.

"I stepped off the train, and it was…overwhelmin'. So busy and big. Everyone hurryin' this way and that. Women all prim and proper, and me there in my trousers and a funny accent. I got some looks, I tell ya."

Carter let out a hearty laugh that ended in a fit of coughs. He quickly pulled the handkerchief to his mouth, covering it with his hand, then stuffed it away to hide the evidence. I gave him a glare that said he didn't fool me none but refrained from further comment. I came to cheer him up, not lecture him.

"I bought a few books. Explored the city. Went to the theatre. Met a few people—some interestin', some unsavory. Three days later, I was back on the train."

"Three whole days, huh?"

"There were opportunities for women, more than I thought. I could've studied to become a doctor, like my father. But..." I took a deep breath and let it slide out slow and easy. "I couldn't run from what I needed to do. So, I went back home. Bought a new gun. Here I am."

"I think you made the right choice."

I turned my gaze out the window to the little town that lay on the other side of the glass. "This feels right. I'm at peace with my choices."

"That's important. You don't want to get to the end and feel otherwise."

With a sideways glance, I analyzed his statement. What did he regret?

He coughed again and wiped his mouth with the back of his hand. A bright speckle of blood covered his skin, and this time he couldn't hide the evidence. Carter eyed me wearily.

We locked in a silent stare until finally he said, "Sarah, even if this don't kill me, I need to retire this badge, and I want to make sure this town is in good hands."

"Carter, I've already told you."

He held up a hand and forced himself to stand up tall. "I know, but this time it's real. I'm tired, and probably a dead man walkin'."

"Don't say that."

"You know as well as I do how this usually ends, not that I ain't holdin' out hope."

"I'm sorry," I shook my head and dipped my eyes to the floor, then looked back up, "but I don't want the badge, Carter. You know I'm here to help with anything, but that…no. You'll have to find someone else."

He rounded his desk and sank into his chair, defeated. "I understand."

"And you know Maggie and the kids have us…*if* you don't pull through, right?"

With a slow, resigned nod, he said, "Thank you."

I moved around the desk and gave him a pat on the shoulder. "Get some rest, Sheriff. There's some oranges in there too. They came in on the train this mornin'. They're good for ya."

"You know, some of us are made from a different metal than others, Sarah. We're the ones that shoulder the load when times get rough. Make the tough choices. Face whatever comes head on. We're the protectors. They need people like us, or the peace falls and innocent people get hurt."

I met his eyes, and without a word, walked out. Safe from view, I turned the corner and fell back against the alley wall. The muscles around my chest constricted until they squeezed a wheezing breath out. His words ran circles through my mind. I understood his concern, but why did it have to be me? I didn't want the responsibility of the badge. Or the danger that came with it. I'd left all that behind.

No. One of his deputies could take the reins. The Doctor had retired. Sarah Sawyer was a rancher now.

Determined to find a distraction, I ventured out to see Darla. I'd heard she and her husband, Jed, could use a hand. Some hard work would do good to soothe the soul. The aging couple happily accepted my offer, and Clover and I set out to the pasture with Jed. By the end of the afternoon, we had mended the fences and stored the hay. Jed headed into town, and I settled on the porch with Darla and some of her famous tea.

"This town nearly perished ten years ago," Darla said out of nowhere, rocking her chair with a faraway look. "Hard times for all."

Every now and then, the old woman would drop nuggets of history when we'd have our front porch chats. While I did love exploring the past in books, firsthand accounts were more entertaining.

"We'd been a flourishin' mining' town until silver started to crash. Sheriff Carter kept the peace when things fell apart."

"He's a good man."

"He is. And strong. But luckily, we were blessed with a bunch of strong women here too." She touched my knee and smiled. "Men think they're the boss of everything, but we both know women hold the power."

I had to laugh at the memory of my mother keeping track of money and making most of the family decisions. "My mother once said she was the brains behind my father's muscle."

Darla cackled.

"What made it even funnier was that my father was a skinny man, a doctor, and not particularly known for his brawn."

"Didn't make it any less true." She gave me a knowing glance. "But that's where Jo comes in. A couple years after the crash, she bought the saloon and turned it into a respectable business. Ran out all the unsavoriness that came with the loss of livelihood. She wasn't afraid to go toe to toe with anyone."

"She is fiery," I said with pride and affection.

"That she is. When people saw what she was doin', well, it changed everything."

I nodded, taking in the history of the town as well as Jo's role in it—something she hadn't revealed, or maybe, didn't understand. Her determination and strength hadn't just been an anchor for me, but for an entire town. I couldn't be more proud to be with her.

"Then Jo brought us you, and you brought Jessie and Jackie and Ann. We've never been better off. Hellfire, we can even vote. And we'll need all of us to get through this coming mess. Life is full of cycles, you know. Ups and downs. We're headed for another down, but we'll make it if we stick together."

"We will."

Cycles…that was the reason I couldn't fully relax. The downside never failed to come back around again, forever leaving me looking over my shoulder.

"All we need now is one of ya to be mayor. Or sheriff," she added with a wink.

And now the reason for this particular story made sense. "I'll be sure to tell them they have your vote if they run," I said, ignoring the sheriff remark.

She regarded me for a long moment, then patted my knee. "You do that."

"I should probably get." I set my empty cup on the small table between us. "Won't be long till sunset, and there's still chores to do back home."

"Appreciate you indulgin' me with a chat, Sarah. I do enjoy the company."

"Anytime."

"Don't work too hard."

"No, ma'am."

She smiled knowingly and waved as I mounted Clover. I tipped my hat and trotted away, anxious to get back to Jo, and the one place no one pushed me to pick up a fight I didn't want.

# CHAPTER FIVE

When I arrived in town the next morning, a crowd gathered at the entrance of the sheriff's office derailed my trip to the bank. As I strode closer, raised voices wrought with concern carried loud enough to hear. My steps quickened. I pushed through the bodies to the front. Ben, Charlie, and Bobby stood flustered, stammering to answer question after question. Carter was nowhere to be found. My worst fear had come true.

Or so I'd thought.

There stood Bobby, all wet behind the ears and baby-faced, with the badge of sheriff pinned to his chest. He looked as if he'd crumble when the wind blew.

My stomach plummeted to the floor. A wave of wooziness washed over me. Was Carter still alive? Who came up with idea of Bobby as sheriff? And were the other two experienced deputies truly such cowards they refused to take charge?

I needed answers. First, we needed everyone to get out.

I caught Ben's attention, and gave him an unmistakable glare that sent him cowering. Nice to know I still had it in me. He quickly straightened himself, and with his deep, booming voice, announced a town hall meeting would be organized and that everyone should go home. Mutterings commenced as the people filtered out. Hushed voices of concern and anger swirled about, but the one that caught my ear came from a young woman who'd arrived a few months ago.

"I thought I'd be safer here," she whispered to the couple beside her. Fear laced her words, and she shrunk away, disappearing into the crowd.

A groan of frustration rumbled through my chest. *Damned cycles. Why'd I have to be right about things going to shit?* No time to wallow. We needed to figure out how to keep the town together.

"Somebody start talkin'," I ordered in a tone that straddled stern and angry.

Silence stretched as they glanced between one another, casting weary looks. Finally, Charlie took a step forward. Looking as if the firing squad stood ten paces away, his face paled. He wrung his hands and choked on his words. How did these three ever get a badge? I knew Carter had been scraping the bottom of the barrel for help but...

A heavy sigh seeped out. Who was I to talk? I didn't want the responsibility either.

I softened my glare a bit. "Just tell me what happened to Carter. No one's gettin' in trouble."

"Okay. Good." Charlie's rigid shoulders relaxed in relief. He sighed and glanced at the other two before saying, "Cause, um, we weren't sure what to do after Carter collapsed."

My heart stumbled a beat. A squeezing in my chest forced a lump up into my throat, but I pushed a single word past the blockage. "When?"

"Late last night. Most of the town was quiet, but a fight broke out at the Partin house, and on his way there, he just collapsed. I was riding with him. I picked him up and rushed him to Doc."

"How is he?" My breath hung in wait for his answer.

"Pretty bad, I think. I helped Doc take him home this mornin'. He wasn't of sound mind at the time."

"Okay," I breathed out. Carter might've been bad off, but there was still a sliver of hope. "Good work." The compliment brought a proud grin to Charlie's face. "And Bobby?" His smile withered. "Why the hell is he sheriff?"

"Well, uh...see," he stiffened once again, "me and Ben got families. W—"

"Families? That's your excuse?" When no answer came, I rolled my eyes and groaned. "You two already wear badges. That's no safer. And you have experience." It took a will of steel to tamp my anger down.

"Sorry, Sarah, but Bobby agreed to take over. We'll teach him."

"Teach him," I muttered under my breath as I threw another glare their way. "Does that help you sleep at night? Does that make you feel safe?"

Done with their nonsense, I stomped out before any reply came, climbed back onto Clover, and raced toward Carter's house.

Maggie answered the door, her eyes weary and exhaustion evident. The sound of cheerful children playing carried throughout the house, a complete contradiction to the theme of the day.

"Hello, Sarah."

"H—How is he?"

"He woke up for a bit, but he's sleeping now. I don't…it's not good." Tears began a slow run down her cheeks. Her shoulders shook, but Maggie, ever the face of quiet strength, quickly composed herself.

She had no reason to hold it in. Not in front of me, anyway. She did plenty of that with her kids and Carter. I rushed forward, wrapping her into a tight hug. She clung to me like a lifeline and let it all go. There was nothing I could do to help Carter, but I could give Maggie a much needed moment of release.

"I got you," I whispered, my hands running comforting circles along her back.

"What am I going to do without him?" she asked, words breaking around heavy sobs.

"You're strong, Maggie. It won't be easy, but you'll make it," I said, still stroking her back. "And you're not alone. You and the kids, you have us."

A shudder wracked Maggie's body during a particularly strong gasp. I held her tighter until she calmed, whispering words of support over and over. When she had cried herself out, she looked up at me with gratitude in her reddened eyes. She pulled away and cleaned herself up, her shaky hands wiping furiously with a yellow handkerchief.

"Thank you, Sarah. I appreciate your friendship. You and Jo and Jessie, all of you, but..." she inhaled a ragged breath, "it's not the same."

"I know." The memory of losing Jo ripped through me. The hole it had put in my chest still took my breath away. But I'd been lucky. My loss had only been temporary. There'd be no happy ending here. "I know," I said again, regretting that she would most likely be feeling that loss far too soon. "Can I see him?"

"Of course."

She led me to their room and opened the door. My breath fell still. Even under the rays of daylight Carter looked pale, so pale, and thin as a rail, cheeks gaunt. The end was near.

# CHAPTER SIX

Two days was all it had taken. As if every unsavory had heard our new sheriff was barely old enough to be considered a man, one ruckus after another had sprung up around our peaceful town. Having passed Ben arresting a man for stealing from the general store, a quivering voice drew my attention to the alleyway. I paused at the edge of the building and peered around the corner.

A rough and tumble stranger, haggard-looking and dust covered, had a gun pointed at old Abe. The man searched Abe's pockets for money and talked about how he'd lost everything after moving out here. Abe's eyes were wide with fear while our new sheriff, with shaky hands and trembling words, made a feeble demand for the thief to stop. Couldn't blame the guy for laughing in Bobby's face, but the arrogance and lack of respect for others brought my temper racing to the surface.

*It's the sheriff's job to handle such matters, not mine,* I repeatedly reminded myself, but that didn't keep my hand from drifting down to my holster.

"Oh yeah, what you gonna do, boy?" the stranger challenged. His full attention shifted to Bobby.

Despite the growing urge to intervene, I held myself back. I truly didn't want to go down that path. Even when the man shoved Abe to the ground, I willed Bobby to toughen up, to be the badge and handle it without me.

"Well...I'm the, uh, the sheriff of this town. I'm gonna take you to jail."

A grumble of annoyance freed itself from the confines of my chest. Bobby was weak. Scared. A boy. He was going to get himself killed.

"C'mon Bobby," I muttered under my breath. Time was running out.

"Are ya now? That's funny." The man stepped closer, dangerous dark eyes narrowing. "Who's gonna listen to the likes of you? Your own dog probably kicks dirt in your face." Another laugh roared out, hearty and proud, as the man continued to close the gap between them.

"I su—suggest y—you leave now, sir." Bobby took a wobbly step backward, hand fumbling for his gun.

"Or what?"

Okay, time to put an end to this mess. I stepped out into the alley behind Bobby.

"Or it'll get ugly for you," I said, low and rumbly, practically a growl.

"What's this? Sheriff's got a woman doin' his work for him?" His loud bark of laughter reeked of condescension. "This gets better and better. Darlin', why don't you leave this boy behind, and I'll show you what a man can do."

*Well, that line never gets old.* I dismissed him with a laugh of disdain.

With a quick step, he shoved Bobby into the wall, and he crumbled to the ground with the fragility of a butterfly. The stranger's smirk transformed into a sneer as he moved closer. He had a lot to say, but he'd be silenced soon enough.

On instinct, my hand went to work, quickly drawing and firing a shot. The bullet struck the tip of his boot. He stopped in his tracks, but I kept my gun drawn.

"Sarah…" Bobby cautioned.

The man's face shifted into something resembling concern, but his cockiness remained. A sudden flare of recognition flashed in his eyes. "You missed, Doc."

The nickname brought an involuntary twitch to my lip. Something deep inside reveled in the fact the Doctor still had a reputation. All warmth escaped the bondage of my skin, leaving a river of ice coursing through my veins, surging into my right arm, and down to the finger teasing the trigger.

"Were you wantin' to die? Cause that can be arranged." I eased the hammer back. The barrel made a slow rise toward his chest.

And just like that, fear oozed from his pores. He dropped Abe's money on the ground and backed away. With my free hand, I dug into my pocket and flicked him a fifty-cent piece. His eyes bloomed when he realized the worth of the coin.

"Get a bite and a bath, anywhere but here. Understood?"

He picked the coin from the ground, then turned and ran away without a word. I resisted the urge to hunt him down, to make sure he didn't bring any more trouble back.

Bobby let out a relieved breath and popped back up onto his feet. "Thanks, Sarah."

I pulled my attention from the retreating form and stared at Bobby. The badge didn't belong on him. I shook my head. "Sorry, Bobby, you're not ready for this."

"I know." Bobby's head hung in shame.

He'd done his best. More importantly, he had tried to be the protector we needed. That was more than I could say for the rest of us. I removed the star from his chest and held it in my hand, staring at the pointed symbol of the law. The warmth of the metal against the cold raging under my skin brewed up a storm of confusing feelings.

Abe moved gingerly, pushing himself up off the ground with creaky knees and a grunt. "Thank you, Sarah."

"It was nothin', Abe. Glad everyone is all right." His fragile old body appeared shaken, but unharmed.

"No offense, Bobby, but that badge is much more suited for Sarah's chest. We appreciate your bravery though."

Bobby perked up a little and said, "I didn't want it, but I was tryin' to help."

"I know. Thanks for that," Abe said. He walked over to me, gently took the badge from my hand, and fixed it to my shirt with tender care. He smiled and patted me on the back. "Have a nice day, Sheriff."

Wordless, I stared down at the shiny star I swore I'd never wear. "Dammit, Carter."

Clover raced at a full gallop back to the ranch. What would Jo think? We'd skimmed the topic several times before. While Jo had said she'd support any decision, I hadn't missed the hesitation in her voice or worry in her eyes. Being sheriff was a noble cause and all, but did anyone ever truly want their loved ones to wear a badge?

The ranch came into view and an uncomfortable lump swelled in my throat. Clover had made good time, better than I would've liked since I still hadn't wrapped my head around accepting the job I had steadfastly declined. I unpinned the star and shoved it into my vest pocket. We slowed from a trot to a walk to cool Clover down but also to buy myself more time.

When we were close enough, I spotted Jo out in the garden, same as when I'd left hours ago. I threw her a wave with no attention to whether or not she'd been looking as I headed to the barn. Hopefully, she wouldn't rush over, as she was apt to do on occasion. I needed all the time I could get before having to deliver the news.

Seemed luck had been on my side. Jo kept busy while I unsaddled Clover and set her up for the night. As I approached the garden though, it became all too apparent that I'd spent more time worrying than strategizing. I patted the dust from my pants and swallowed thickly, mouth dry, and absent of words. Jo stood and waved, her happiness at my return evident in every bit of her demeanor. I tipped my hat, held up a finger to say I'd be back, then darted into the house to gather my wits. I shut the door behind me and took a deep breath, my mind running through a hundred different scenarios.

"Such a damned coward. How can I wear this badge?"

My alone time lasted but seconds before Jo raced in, worry erasing all joy. I hated the look, but I hated even more so being the reason.

"What's wrong?" she asked, caution causing her voice to waver.

"Why would anything be wrong?"

"Sarah…" That stern tone always did the trick.

I reached into my pocket, pulled out the badge, and tossed it onto the kitchen table. Jo stared, slack-jawed, at a loss for words. Seconds, minutes, who could say how long we stood there with Jo looking at the badge, then at me, and back again. Finally, she shook her head, confusion plain as day, and set her hands on her hips.

"What does this mean?"

"It means I'm the new sheriff."

Her blank expression was almost as intimidating as her angry one, and having no idea what else to say set me on edge.

"Wha…?" Jo shook her head. "Why? How? I thought…?"

"I didn't. I don't." A heavy breath forced itself from my lungs. I yanked off my hat and tossed it on the table beside the badge. Fingers, usually steady and certain, fumbled their way through my hair. I avoided looking Jo in the eye, but after another breath, I did exactly that and said, "It has to be me. At least for now."

"But why? Surely, there's someone else. Maybe one of the new folks can do it?"

"Damn sure ain't Bobby. You shoulda seen how he crumbled under the pressure, all stumblin' and shakin'. Almost got himself killed. Do you honestly want to trust what we've all built to a wet-behind-the-ears boy or a stranger with unknown loyalties? These people moving here, filling up our town, don't know what they're getting themselves into. Am I supposed to trust them to take care of all of us when they might not be able to take care of their own?"

Jo sighed and shook her head. Her hands fell slack at her sides as she looked away. "I know." She closed the distance between us, arms looping around my waist and pulling our bodies flush. "There's no doubt you're the best person for the job. You're strong and skilled, tough, but fair, and everyone likes you. They trust you. But I'll worry about you. Wearing that star could bring more trouble than our pasts ever did."

Those hazel eyes staring into mine held another unspoken concern, one that looked primed to become heard. Instead, she pressed a kiss to my lips.

"I know." I stole a second kiss and inhaled the heavenly scent of Jo. "I worry too, but I'll be extra careful. Like I've said before, my sole purpose each day is gettin' back to you."

"You better."

Jo released her hold, much to my dismay. She picked up the badge and stared at it for a long moment before turning and pinning it to my vest. Stepping back to admire it, a small smile broke through the tight, pursed lips she'd held since she'd heard the news.

"Looks good on you, Sheriff."

A half-smile quirked the corner of my mouth. Most people would probably be happy to don the star. A small part of me did feel the honor of it all, but mostly, I had a strong sense of loyalty to Carter and the town. I wanted to protect the place I'd come to call home and the people who'd become family, even outside the boundaries of our ranch.

"Just promise me you won't try to do it all yourself. You have help. You have support and, if needed, guns."

"I promise. And as soon as someone honorable enough comes along, I'll step down."

Jo forced a smile, but we both understood that might take a while.

# CHAPTER SEVEN

"Don't you worry, Sarah, I'll take care of dem chores." The cowboy's dark skin wore creases that spoke of his life's trials but didn't steal from his wide, pearly white smile. Pride shone in George's chestnut eyes. And with good reason. A young boy when he gained his freedom from slavery, George set out to build a life far away from those memories. He took a grueling job laying the tracks for railroads until he found a place to call home. We were fortunate to snap him up when he settled here. Someone honest to a fault who worked as hard as me was a rare find. Now, he was our farm foreman.

George adjusted his hat and looked around. "Anything else you be needin'?"

"Not that I can think of. Thank you, George. Don't know what I'd do without ya."

"Never get a night's sleep with all the work to be done," he answered with a grin.

A laugh could not be denied. "You speak the truth. Was gettin' close to it."

"I'm glad Jo made you hire help."

I narrowed my eyes, to which he smiled wider. Yes, everyone knew only Jo could talk sense into me, but still, I liked to imagine I was in charge. "How about you bring the family over for supper later?"

"Look forward to it."

I tipped my hat and wished him a good day. George rode away on his bay mustang, Brandy, who he'd found near death and nursed back to health. Much like me and Clover, they were fast friends. His posture confident and relaxed as if he'd been born in the saddle, I'd never met a more natural horseman. Hard to believe he'd only taken it up a year and a half ago.

As if sensing my moment of nostalgia, Clover nudged me, and I kissed her behind the ear. I finished with the saddle and mounted up. When we left the barn, I spotted Jessie tying up her horse. Her long stride took no time for her to reach my side. She stopped on a dime at the sight of the star.

"Never thought I'd see the day." Jessie perched her hands on her hips and stared up at me.

"You're not the only one."

"You sure about this?" She fixed me with a steely gaze that meant business.

"Nope."

"Can I talk you out of it?"

"Not unless you're interested in takin' over."

"Nope."

"Figured as much."

She let out a soft chuckle. "But you know I've got your back. Anytime, anywhere. Despite what I said before."

"I know, and I appreciate that, but you're retired. Gotta get some new folks involved."

She nodded. "Word of advice?"

"Sure."

"Don't be the Doctor. This isn't revenge or teachin' lessons. This is the law. If they ain't breakin' it, you can't go breakin' them."

"I'll do my best." Easier said than done.

"Off you go then. Be careful, Sheriff."

I tipped my hat and nudged Clover forward, hoping my first day would be a quiet one.

Nearly everyone had crammed themselves into the small meeting place. Face after recognizable face, men and women of all ages and races stood shoulder to shoulder, reinforcing the pride I felt at being a part of the town.

Sighs of relief mixed with the murmurs of questions bubbled up when I stepped onto the stage wearing the badge. The mayor took his place at the podium and formally announced I had taken the reins as sheriff. A few called for a vote, but with no one else willing to accept the position, their suggestion was moot. Otherwise, the support had been overwhelmingly positive, which touched me in a way I hadn't expected. The last few weeks had been quite the emotional eye-opener regarding my place in the world. Somehow, I had managed to become a key cog in the wheel.

Mom and Dad would be proud.

Fighting a smile, I stepped to the podium and outlined a plan that involved community help in keeping things in order. Despite the lack of interest in becoming sheriff, no shortage of hands raised in volunteer of taking up watches. Everyone agreed to keep an eye out and report anything out of the ordinary. I even rustled up a couple more deputies, young men by the names of Sam and Cody. By the end of the meeting, most seemed satisfied with the plan of action. Tomorrow we'd start to see how it would all unfold.

We'd managed one peaceful day. The next day, however, came my first test. Between another newspaper article touting how murderous the Indians were and the horse's ass a few seats down working my last nerve, my relaxing supper break was short-lived. Jo had been as tactful and polite as possible, for as long as possible. Though she tried to keep from making a scene, he continually refused to pay and get gone. The tall, stocky cowboy with an unfamiliar accent seemed to take delight in both his defiance and his crude comments to the ladies. I'd long since learned to let Jo handle the usual ruckus, but I drew the line at the blatant disrespect on display. Not only toward Jo, but the town too—my town.

At his last outburst of colorful language, I hit my limit. I gulped down the rest of my beer, then adjusted my hat. Turning with full scowl in force and badge flashing, I growled, "I think it's best you leave now. You're not welcome here anymore. That includes the rest of this town too."

"A woman sheriff. A woman business owner. This town needs a few real men to come in and remind you of your place." He laughed, proud of himself, but when he looked around the room, no one else shared his amusement. His smile faded.

"Not another one," I grumbled under my breath. My lips twitched, and just as fast, I had both guns pointed squarely at his chest. "I've got a place for ya. Right next to the other men who tried to show me my place."

"You know, I'm surprised they let killers wear a badge."

The clench of my jaw matched the slow draw of pressure on the triggers. His eyes grew wide, and despite bowing up, the smell of fear wafted from him.

Jade stepped between us, forcing me to ease off. Frustration drove my teeth to grind. "Jade, step aside. I'll take care of this."

"I have no doubt, but maybe this can be taken outside," she suggested.

"Jade, what are you doin'?" Jo hissed, concerned and irritated.

"We finally got the place back together after the Mitchell twins wrecked it all to Hell." She argued. "I'm just protecting what's ours."

"I'm not breakin' nothin'," he said. "Just havin' a drink and some fun." Jade let out a yelp when he pulled her back toward him. "Have some fun with me."

"Dammit, Jade," Jo groaned. "Sarah…" The slightest of quivers gave way as she said my name—a pleading, or perhaps a warning.

I didn't flinch. Didn't respond. My eyes locked with the defiant stranger's in a battle of wills I refused to lose.

"Let her go and get the hell out now. Final warnin'." Anger sprung up like a summer squall. Everything I had worked hard to lock away had found a key and now wrestled to get free.

"Or what? You'll shoot me? Doubtful with her in the way." He positioned himself behind Jade. A mistakenly placed victorious grin spread across his face.

"She's done it before," Jade reminisced with a wince. "Got the scar to prove it and the ache in my shoulder every time it rains as a reminder."

I took great satisfaction in the way his cocky grin dwindled, and my own grew wider at his discomfort. The key to my inner darkness turned, allowing the door to crack open. The Doctor's need to set the man straight began to slowly slip over me like a fog.

"But now you wear a badge." He swallowed hard. His eyes darted from me to Jade to the swinging doors, considering his options. "You have to play by the rules." Nervous tension now shook in his voice. "You wouldn't shoot an unarmed man."

"You've got two arms, and you're usin' them to hold her hostage." I tipped my head to the right and a pop loosened my neck. A wicked smirk rolled up, replacing the easy grin.

"Wouldn't look good for a woman sheriff to buck the law. Only proves why you shouldn't wear the star in the first place," he rationalized, a desperate plea.

"You wanna test that theory?"

Nick jumped up, his eyes glued to Jade. Worry set his fingers to fidgeting. "No one's more worthy of that star than Sheriff Sawyer," he said. "We approve of any method she deems necessary to deal with the likes of you."

A dozen other men stood at his words to show their support. A few cowered under tables. The women in the room all donned smiles of some sort, be it cautious or proud. Out the corner of my eye, I caught Mrs. Jones reaching around the edge of the bar to pull out the shotgun. She cocked it and aimed at his back. The room went deadly silent.

A grave expression fell over his face.

"That's right," Mrs. Jones chimed in. "You better choose quick. Leave now or get dead. You're cuttin' into my poker time." Her words were sharp, spoken with zero nonsense like a mother scolding a child.

Took a will of iron to fight back a laugh, but deep inside, I felt the shift. Hibernation was over. The Doctor was ready to feast.

"Today's as good as any to get back to my murderous ways." Eyes narrowing, I instinctively zoned in on my mark to the point all I could see was the middle button on his vest. Dead center sounded good.

"Y'all are crazy."

"That we are, now let go of her and get out," Nick yelled, his anger and concern growing. "I'll pay your tab if you promise to stay away for good."

The man shoved Jade away and took off like a jackrabbit. Quick reflexes sent my arm out to keep her from falling to the ground. "You okay?" I asked, eyes tracking the stranger until he disappeared from sight.

"Si. Just happy you didn't shoot me again."

"I'll do my best to avoid usin' that option, but that one woulda been all on you." Though I gave Jade a smile, my insides growled. The temptation to hunt him down continued to build. My fingers twitched, and my feet begged to move, to find and eliminate the threat. Or what he might bring back.

Jade laughed, no inkling of my inner turmoil as I forced my guns back into my holster. Nick appeared at our side. He gave me a nod, then focused all of his concern on Jade. Mrs. Jones tossed me a grin as she took her seat back at the poker table. The crowd returned to their activities as if nothing had happened.

I couldn't do the same.

Everything felt personal with the star pinned to my chest. Everyone's safety rested in my hands. It had been one thing to take on a threat by choice, but now my duty and responsibility extended beyond that of my own circle. The badge carried a heavier weight than I'd expected, giving me a deeper appreciation for Carter's years of service.

"I don't find this increase in newcomers stirrin' up trouble amusin'," Jo grumbled, whisking away Jade's smile. "What're we gonna do?"

"I'll take care of it," I said, again sending my glare at the swinging doors, begging him to have the gall to walk back in. Steely determination had set up camp, and I welcomed the return of the cold. I couldn't deny the strength and comfort I found under the guise of the Doctor.

"Remember, you don't have to do it alone." Jo's warm palm pressed against my cheek. Through a haze of fluttering eyelashes, I moved to meet Jo's worried gaze. "You have me. And all of them, Sarah."

When I glanced around the room, more than a few sets of eyes met mine. A couple of hats tipped. I did have them. Their backing brought about a sense of comfort, but when it came time for action, with or without their help, I'd protect this town to the end.

# CHAPTER EIGHT

With Jo by my side, we knocked on the wooden door to Carter's house. The door creaked open to Maggie, frail and worn out with dark circles under red, puffy eyes. Over the last few days, Carter had taken a downward turn. While Doc didn't believe it to be Consumption, death had a hold of him with both claws.

"Thank you for coming. I sent the kids to Mrs. Davis. He doesn't have long."

She ushered us inside and into the bedroom, where a ghostly pale Carter lay in bed, staring out the open window. A light breeze filtered in. At the sound of our footsteps, he turned and offered a tired smile. Silver hairs had claimed rule of his once dark moustache.

"Howdy, ladies." The words came weak and breathless.

"Hello, Carter," Jo said with a tremble at the end despite her steady and strong demeanor.

When he caught sight of the star on my chest, his smile crept higher. A brief shine lit his eyes, then faded. His gaze worked slowly upward to meet mine, seemingly taking all of his energy.

With a humorless chuckle, I said, "You won, Carter."

"I knew I would," he rasped. His smile shifted into the cocky smirk we all knew so well.

A small laugh tumbled out of Jo. Her hand pressed against my back. Maggie stood silent. She pulled a wet cloth from a bowl, squeezed it out, and pressed it to his head.

I stepped forward and knelt beside him. "I promise to keep this town and our families safe. To wear the badge proudly, like you did."

"Thank you, Sarah. I have no d—" *Cough. Cough.* "Doubt you will." A wheezy exhale flowed past his lips. "We're made of the same metal, remember?" His hand covered mine, and when I nodded, he gave it a squeeze. A tear rolled from the corner of his eye as he looked to Jo. "Take good care of her."

"I will." Jo's reply slipped past quivering lips.

Then he settled his gaze on Maggie, remaining there as a strained breath forced its way out of his lungs. He pulled his hand away and reached up for hers. "I love you," he said, voice growing faint. "I love our kids. Thank you for g—giving me the best life a man could ask for."

Maggie's knuckles whitened as her grip grew tighter—a last attempt to keep him from leaving her. A sharp sob echoed through the room. Jo and I moved aside for Maggie to sit beside him. Again, Jo's arm found a home against my back, this time pulling me closer. The erratic breath of

Jo's suppressed cries filled my ears, but no tears fell. Peace could be found in the fact a man of the law would leave this world on his own accord.

Some might find it unjust a man as strong as Carter would perish by the hand of illness rather than a bullet. I believed otherwise. He had survived, beaten all comers, and lived to the fullest. Everyone would meet their end one day. To do so with loved ones around you, absent of violence, was the best anyone could hope for.

His chest fell still, breath silent. Blank eyes stared up into nothing, but a hint of a smile lingered. Maggie's shrill scream of pain ripped throughout the eerie quiet of the house. Jo rushed to her side, engulfing Maggie in her arms before she could fall to the floor.

I stared at him a moment, my heart stuttering at the loss of a good man and a good friend, before I pulled the sheet up over his head. As I sucked in a shaky breath, a momentary thought struck—how many more breaths would I be lucky enough to take?

I quickly chased the question away. There was work to be done.

"Rest now, Carter. I'll shoulder the load."

It was a sunny morning on the twenty-third of July when we laid Carter Hamilton to rest. Hundreds turned out to say their goodbyes to a man who'd helped so many and given so much. Not usually one to give a speech, the loss of a close friend had moved me to say a few words. I'd hoped to bring some comfort to Maggie, her kids, and in some small way, to myself. For the most part, it had worked. I felt lighter, and Maggie had offered an appreciative smile, but we all knew it would be short lived. She would go home with a hole in her heart and a house full of memories from their lives together. We'd go our separate ways with an emptiness in our chests and intangible flashes of moments spent with our friend.

Like the time he called me out as the Doctor as if knowing my secret would push me away from Jo. That smug little grin of his under that damned mustache had irked me to no end, but my staying had irked him every bit as bad. Our relationship had started with a stalemate but soon grew into a fond friendship. When he'd offered to deputize me during the search for Jo, his gesture had been appreciated, but I'd had no intentions of obeying any laws in the hunt to find her. He'd understood my defiance then, and now he trusted me to carry on his legacy. I wouldn't let him down.

"Maggie, are you sure you won't come stay a few more days? It's no problem," Jo asked again, and for the fifth time, Maggie declined. She and the kids had stayed with us for the last three days.

"We'll have to face it sooner or later, Jo, but thank you both so much for your hospitality. I'm grateful for your friendship."

"Anything you need, anytime day or night, just holler, okay?" I said, leaving no question she would ever be an inconvenience.

"I will, Sarah."

After a hug for each of them, Jo wrapped her arm around my waist, and we watched them climb into their wagon to make the sad trek home. Words didn't exist to adequately describe the emptiness of loss they'd have to endure, but I knew it well. I took a moment to mourn their journey ahead, then turned my focus on my present and the comfort that came from the warm arm of the strong woman beside me. Jo leaned in and pressed a kiss to the corner of my jaw. Like butter over a flame, I melted into her.

"Let's go home," she said. The urging press of her arm against my hip got us moving. "I want to snuggle up with you for the rest of the day. Can we do that?"

I met her eyes, glimmering with overflowing love but tinged with an underlying fear of loss. I knew the feeling well. I hated seeing it in Jo, regretted that I'd be putting it there again. Probably sooner than I'd like.

"Yeah." I slung my arm over her shoulder and pulled her tight to me as we walked. "We can do that."

# CHAPTER NINE

The mischief had quieted down a bit. Fights were at a minimum and reports of thefts had lessened, thanks to our group watches. The lack of confrontation had given me a chance to calm down, get my bearings, and reconcile the darkness roiling inside. Wearing the badge required a delicate balance. One I had wanted no part of before, but one I had now accepted and needed to gain a grasp on. The troubles plaguing nearby towns, however, made it difficult to settle. My guard and my protective streak on edge, even the slightest disturbance had me reaching for my gun.

"Howdy, Sheriff," the familiar voice with a cocky edge stirred me from the depths of thought.

"Jessie. What brings you by?"

"I heard you thinkin'," she said, laughing as she stepped fully inside the office.

"Thought you said I didn't do that kinda thing."

"Guess that's why the rusty ol' gears were screamin' so loud then."
We shared a laugh and she took the seat across the desk. "How's it goin'?"

"Quiet. For now."

"Good to hear. How are you?"

"Workin' on that."

She nodded, seeming to understand exactly what I'd meant. "And Jo?"

"Also quiet. For now." A smile came with the look she gave me.
Would only be a matter of time before Jo snapped. "She's...as you'd
expect."

"Yeah." Jessie rubbed the back of her neck and looked away. "Jackie's
worried too, but you know, glad I didn't take the job."

"Understandable."

"I guess so, though I feel like it shoulda been me. I have the
experience."

I leaned back in my chair and mulled over her words until I came to
a conclusion. "Maybe, but some part of me believes this is where I'm
meant to be. At least for now."

"Who'da thunk?" A chuckle trickled out.

Before I could say anything else, another familiar face popped in.
"Ann?"

"Hello, Sarah."

I rose from my seat and rushed to greet her. "I haven't seen you in
ages. Where've you been?"

Her arms wrapped around me in a warm embrace. "Went to see
family. Seems I've missed some things here though." When she pulled

away, she ran her fingers across my badge. "Sorry to hear about Carter." Ann looked up at me, sadness gleaming in her eyes.

"Yeah. Thanks. Um…yeah. We uh, plan to go check up on Maggie tonight."

"I'll be sure to go see her soon. Maybe watch the kids and let her have a break."

"Would be good for the kids too. I'll ask her."

"Great. Well, I'll let you ladies get back to it. We'll catch up soon. I promise." She shot me a smile. "And that," Ann pointed to the badge, "looks good on you," she added with a wink.

"Why, thank ya, ma'am." I tipped my hat. She laughed as she walked away.

Jessie rolled her eyes. "I'm gonna tell Jo you've been sweet talkin' the ladies again."

"And here I thought you were my best friend."

"I am. That's why I gotta make sure you don't mess up."

"Oh? So that's wh—"

"Sheriff!" Denny, the farrier's boy, rushed through the door. "Come quick. Marvin and Junior is fightin' at the store."

"Why this time?" Jessie asked, neither surprised nor amused.

"Same as always. Pearl," he said, then ran back out.

"Those two…" I rushed outside, Jessie hot on my heels.

The two young men rolled in the dirt, trading punches and obscenities. They say women make men do crazy things. Neither of those boys needed any help, but the battle for Pearl's affections had sure tipped them both over the edge. The poor girl stood off to the side, begging them to stop.

"All right, break it up, fellas." My sharp, no-nonsense tone did the trick as they quickly parted and sprung to their feet. Red-faced and dirty, they dusted themselves off and collected their hats.

"Sheriff," Marvin started, "I—"

"To my office. Now. Both of ya." The glare I imparted on them left no room for negotiation.

"Yes, ma'am," they answered dutifully as one, then slowly plodded away.

I softened when I turned to Pearl. "I'll need you to come along too," I said, then added in my gentlest tone, "If you don't mind."

"It's okay. Sorry for the trouble." She cast her eyes downward in shame.

"Unless you have a role in this, it's not you who needs to apologize." She peered back up and gave me a soft smile.

"You need any help with this?" Jessie asked.

"Nah."

"Good. I'm gonna go check on that order of seed then." Jessie gave the dust-covered young men an unimpressed once-over before heading up the street.

Pearl and I followed behind the pair until we reached the privacy of the sheriff's office. I shut the door behind us, walked to the front, and pulled a chair out for Pearl. She sat down in silence, refusing to look either of them in the eye. Folding my arms across my chest, I looked the boys up and down and gathered my thoughts. This was one of those times where brawn and bullets were of no use, one of those times I'd have to learn to navigate as each newfound responsibility presented itself.

"Now, who wants to go first?"

Marvin and Junior looked at one another. Since neither wanted to volunteer, I chose, setting my sights hard on Marvin. "You were so talkative earlier, you get to start."

"Well, I uh…"

"Yes?"

"I was talkin' to Pearl and he interrupted and—"

"I wanted to pay my bill," Junior broke in to plead his case. "And you were tryin' to ask her to dinner when she clearly has no interest in you. I was doin' her a favor."

"Pearl," I turned my attention to the young woman once again, "I'm gonna ask you a question. I apologize if it's of a personal nature." With great reluctance, she nodded. "Are you at all interested in havin' dinner, or any other outin', with either of these fine gentlemen?" I made sure the sarcastic emphasis on the last two words had not been missed by either Marvin or Junior. Judging by their demeanor, I'd made my point.

"No, ma'am," she responded softly, her cheeks red with embarrassment as she turned her eyes to the floor.

I stared at Pearl and waited for any change of heart. When none came, I turned back to the young men again. "Seems there's no more reason for you two to be fightin' then. I suggest you both leave Pearl, and one another, alone. Understood?" The steeled expression I leveled at them fell one step shy of deadly.

"Yes, Sheriff Sawyer," they muttered in unison.

"Sorry, Pearl," Junior said, then bowed his head and shuffled out.

Marvin did the same, exiting the opposite direction onto the street. With any luck, that would be the last time those boys bothered Pearl, though I suspected it wouldn't be the last time they'd tangle.

"Thank you, Sarah. They don't listen when I tell them no."

I laughed, knowing that had someone else been after Jo's affections, I'd have done the same. Luckily, Jo had wanted me too. That luck wasn't in the cards for Marvin or Junior with Pearl.

"I'm actually smitten with Bobby," she admitted softly as if it were a secret. Maybe it was, but I'd seen him sneak peeks at her too.

"Bobby is a fine young man."

"Even if he couldn't cut it as sheriff?"

Is that what held her back? Embarrassment? Being sheriff was no easy job. Bobby was far too nice to handle the harshness that came with wearing the badge. Heck, most were.

"Absolutely. He has a kind heart, too kind for what this job entails. And he has eyes for you too, by the way." Pearl looked adorable with her shy grin, the coloring of her cheeks going from white to rose. "Okay, I'll let you go back about your day then. Let me know if you have any more problems with those two, and be sure to talk to Bobby. He's a bit shy."

"Thanks. I'll try. I get a bit tongue-tied around him."

I smiled and gave her a pat on the shoulder as she rose to her feet. Once she'd left, I stood guard over the street until she made it back to the store. These were the kind of problems I'd rather handle. Unfortunately, the ones looming on the horizon wouldn't be as easy to solve.

# CHAPTER TEN

Another column in the paper highlighting growing turmoil in the area sent me on a trip to the neighboring town of Hailey to see how they were doing. I tied Clover up and glanced around. Looked pretty much like my town, but then, round these parts, they all looked much the same. The door to the sheriff's office stood open and I stepped inside.

"Well, I'll be. If it isn't Sheriff Sarah Sawyer." The man in the black hat behind the desk hopped to his feet and strode toward me with a wide grin. "I'm Sheriff Max Herndon. Nice to meet ya." He shook my hand and waved me toward a seat in his office. "I've heard lots of stories," he added with a laugh.

"I can imagine," I said, a grin on my lips that hovered between cocky and genuine. "People like to talk."

"That they do. But I was never one to put much stock in talk."

"Glad to hear." I had a good feeling about Max the moment I saw him. He looked to be about my age, with features slightly worn in a way that spoke of experience. Sincerity shone in his bright green eyes. When I took a seat, he circled around his desk.

"Sorry to hear about Carter." He settled into his chair across from me, a grim look upon his face. "And I can guess what brings you down our way." Max leaned back, clasping his hands on his lap. "Things have been gettin'…tense."

"Yeah, I've heard a few things. I also don't put much stock in talk. Figured I'd come down and hear from you myself. I need to be prepared, and for that, I need facts."

"Hopin' it won't come to much," he said, forcing a smile to take shape.

"The East is no longer happy with what they have. That can only lead to problems for us," I said, glancing around the room to find the wanted posters. "The West is growin'. Changin'. There's no goin' back."

"I suppose you're right. We've already had more robberies than ever, but we've had a few killin's too, and houses on the outskirts raided. A couple people said they'd seen Indians leavin' a burnin' house. The family was dead, their livestock taken." A hardened expression cut through his façade.

A heavy feeling of unease settled in my gut. "That just doesn't sound right. We've had peace with the surroundin' tribes for years."

"I know, but they've had a rough go the last few years with the government redistributin' their land. Maybe it forced their hand? Or maybe they had a debt to settle with that family?"

"Maybe. Still don't sit right with me though. They're proud people who respect our agreement. I can't see them takin' that kind of action.

Unless, like ya said, bein' forced from their land made them desperate. Everyone has their limits."

He shook his head, clearly at a loss. "All I know is everyone's got an eye out for them, already placin' the blame without real proof. I'm doin' what I can to figure it all out. But between the robberies, fights, and drunks, I'm spread pretty thin. Hirin' new deputies is hard. No one wants to get involved."

"I understand. Uncertainty breeds fear, and it spreads like a plague. I want to venture out a bit, see what I can find, try to get to the truth of it all."

"Be careful. I know you're more than capable, but the West has never been more dangerous."

I nodded again and reached into my vest pocket to pull out drawings of the two men I'd dealt with in town. I set them on the table and spread them out. "Either of these men familiar to ya?"

He looked them over, paused in thought. His hand went to the one on the right, the man from the alleyway. "This fella looks kinda like the one that tried to rob the saloon. But the other...I don't know. Maybe, but it's not strikin' a chord. There's been talk of a small gang makin' a name for themselves. Maybe they're related."

"Could be." Seemed I had more questions than answers now. "Thanks for your time, Max."

"Anytime. How about ya bend an elbow with me before you head back?"

"I could definitely use a drink. I also need to stop at the store before I go."

"I'll show you the way."

Having eyes on me was nothing new, but it had been a while since they'd been accompanied by the apprehensive, hushed-whispers that had long since lost their luster at home. When would a woman with a gun not have the effect of a major spectacle? Or a woman with a badge?

Max cast a worried side-eye glance. Did he fear my infamous temper might rear its ugly head? Not today. At least, not for this. The town's people were cautious, and given the current events, caution was warranted.

I tipped my hat to an older couple crossing the street. Their eyes darted down to my gun, moved to my badge, and back up, not quite making eye contact. The man returned the nod, but the grip on his wife's arm tightened. Hailey was busier and more spread out than home, but from what I'd seen, the age of its inhabitants was a bit older. Maybe that's what made it an easier target. Plus, they didn't have the benefit of having three of the West's deadliest women living there.

"They're good people here. Just scared," Max said soft and low, where no one could hear. Seeds of doubt could be as bad as fear.

"Understandable."

"I was raised here. Mom and Pop still live up on the hill. I want to protect them, all of them," he said as we stepped into the saloon. "Keep this town safe for the kids I hope to have one day."

He led me to the front, and we claimed two stools at the end of the bar. The establishment looked more run down than Jo's. It had seen its share of seasons. A heavyset balding man with two teeth missing in his smile made his way over, giving the sheriff a familiar nod, then turning a curious brow towards me.

"A whiskey for me, Poe," the Sheriff said. He looked my way, and I gave him a short nod. "And one for Sheriff Sawyer."

"Comin' right up."

Poe gave us both a wide grin as he reached for a bottle. He quickly poured the two glasses and set them in front of us. I downed my drink in one go. Max took his a bit slower.

"If we work together," I said, an idea coming together. "Get a few towns to team up, we can accomplish that. At the very least, make it harder, then maybe whoever is stirrin' up trouble will go someplace that's easier pickin's. Despite my reputation, I'd prefer to keep the bloodshed at a minimum."

He laughed and threw back the rest of his drink. "Me too. Let me know when you're ready. I know you're just gettin' settled in. I could even come to you. Been a while since I've taken a trip to the mountains."

"Stop by anytime. Got a room for ya." Ready to get back home, I stood and shook his hand. "Thanks for your hospitality, Sheriff. I'll be seein' ya soon."

"You will. Get home safely."

Always my goal, but first... "Which way to the store?"

"Go out, head right. It's three down on your left."

"Appreciate it. Have a good night."

Out the swinging doors and down the street I went. Our towns weren't too far apart, but surely they had some different goods in stock. I couldn't possibly go home without a little something for Jo. Not on our special night. I greeted the clerk on my way in and slowly roamed the shelves. Not much grabbed my eye until I arrived at the case up front. Right away, I knew.

"I'll take that one."

The clerk smiled as he pulled my selection out and wrapped it in plain paper. Jo was going to love it.

# CHAPTER ELEVEN

Rather than head to town, I went straight home. Night had fallen, but Jo wouldn't be back for another couple of hours. Once Clover had been tended to, and the livestock had been fed, I went in search of some twine to use as a bow for Jo's gift. Luckily, it didn't take too much to find a decent looking strand. I cut what I needed and headed in to clean myself up. Maybe I'd have time to prepare a meal too. If everything went as planned, she could come home, relax, and we could enjoy the rest of the night wrapped up in one another.

When Jo finally arrived, her eyes grew wide at the two plates of beef, potatoes, and bread on the table beside her gift. Funny how our appetites differed. I was more excited by the black dress that hugged her tight around the waist with gold trim that brought out the golden flecks in her eyes.

"You went all out, Sarah." Jo moved in close and pressed a soft kiss to my lips. "Thank you." She cupped the angle of my jaw and brushed her thumb lovingly across my cheek.

"You deserve it," I said, eyelids fluttering, fingers fighting the itch to grab her and skip dinner altogether.

Jo flashed me her all-knowing smile. She reached into her bag and pulled out a gift of her own. The package was much bigger and wrapped far nicer in shiny red cloth with a gold bow. I instantly wished I'd put more effort into my wrapping.

"Don't even think it," Jo said, reading my mind. "You know I don't care about appearances. I'm sure it's a thoughtful gift that will make me think of you. You could just as soon wrap it in newspaper. In fact," she continued as she set the gift on the table, "you didn't have to get me anything at all. I have all I need."

"I know, but I wanted to. I saw it and knew you'd love it."

"Well, I love you for thinkin' of me."

"Always, Jo." Ugh, that smile. It got me every time. "Now, come on. Let's eat before it gets cold."

Jo set her coat and bags aside and made her way to the table. She bypassed her seat in favor of wrapping her arms around my waist and snuggling in beneath my chin.

"Can you believe it's been six years since we met?" she breathed out against my skin.

"No." Six years wasn't all that long, but I had a hard time imagining a time without Jo. "Time sure moves quickly, even when it feels like I've known you for ages."

"Yeah." A tense moment of silence fell between us before she spoke again, soft and careful. "I hope we get many more years."

"We will," I assured her and tightened my hold. I pressed a reassuring kiss to her head. If I had any say in it, we would grow old and gray together.

"I worry. Even somethin' as simple as goin' to town. That badge makes you a target."

"I'll be fine." What else could I say? Promises couldn't be made, but I knew how to be careful. Besides, couldn't be any worse than all the other targets I'd had on my back over the years. "As long as we're together, everything will be fine." And I believed that deep down in my soul.

She tipped her head up and met my lips. Kissing Jo was one of the things I loved most about life. Kissing Jo, sunsets, and riding Clover.

Never took much for me and Jo to lose ourselves—hands roaming, tongues searching, hearts racing—until air, or more often than I'd like, interruption, parted us. But not tonight. Tonight we were free to indulge however we pleased, and I planned to enjoy an entire night of her.

Restraining our desires, we slowly unraveled ourselves and enjoyed our meal. Small talk and soft touches made my heart flutter—simple ones, like a stroke down my arm or a squeeze on my knee—I enjoyed Jo's hands on me in any way possible.

Food gone and plates cleaned, we settled side by side in front of the fire and exchanged our gifts. With tender care, I removed the wrapping until the present inside was revealed. My jaw dropped in awe at the new dark brown saddlebags with my initials engraved on the flap.

"Wow, Jo! This is beautiful." The pockets were deep and offered plenty of storage.

"I know you love your old ones, but they're on their last leg."

I leaned over and pecked a kiss to her lips. "I love it. Thank you." My fingers skimmed across the supple leather in admiration. I gently set it down to hand Jo her gift. "Your turn." I couldn't wait to see her face.

Jo tore the paper open faster than a child at Christmas. Her hazel eyes grew wide as a full moon as her hands caressed the pearl handle. "It matches your guns," she said, full of adoration as she felt the weight of the six-inch blade in her hand. "And it's perfectly balanced too. Thank you."

"You're welcome."

"Old Faithful might be mad if I retire her," she said with a laugh. The knife she had religiously kept on her at all times had gouges in the handle and nicks in the metal from a long life of service. "This will give me one more reason to think of you, especially when it's strapped to my thigh."

The temperature suddenly rose, especially in my cheeks. "Aw jeeze, Jo."

Her head fell back in a raucous laugh. "You love it." She rubbed her hand up and down my thigh, bringing warmth to areas other than my heart.

"I do. I love you. Always you. Thank you for these last six years. They've been better than anything I could have dreamed." Love-filled tears pricked my eyes.

"I'm happy to hear that." She cupped my cheek and looked me in the eye. "And I'm so very happy I have you."

I worked my arm around Jo's waist to pull her closer and wrap her up tight. We relaxed in one another's embrace until the fire dimmed, then made our way hand in hand to bed. Only one thing could make the evening any more perfect. The thought had no sooner crossed my mind before agile fingers were undoing my buttons one by one. She brushed the shirt off my shoulders and let it land in a heap at my feet. Patches of skin puckered into those exciting little bumps as her fingertips grazed across my skin.

I deemed it unacceptable being the only one topless. Gently, I turned her and pulled the laces of her corset free. She relieved herself of the dress, spun around, and captured my lips in a kiss that spoke of the fiery need burning between us. I dipped down, pressing wet kisses across her breasts, smiling into them at the sound of her wanting moans as we rid ourselves of our remaining garments.

Jo was still as eager to have me as I her. The proof lay in every scorching touch, each searing kiss. In her eyes shone nothing but love. There would be many more challenges ahead, certainly with the badge on my chest, but with Jo by my side, we would always triumph.

The pureness of it all spurred something inside, a need to feel the truth against every inch of my skin like a comforting bath. Breast to breast, I lifted her up, and as we tumbled onto the bed, I let all things Jo wash over me. The heat of her body beneath mine. The shudder of her breath under my touch. How she gasped out my name between strokes. Her desire coating my fingertips wet and hot. Powerful as the swell of an ocean wave, she swept all other cares away.

Everything else could wait until tomorrow. Tonight, there was only Jo.

# CHAPTER TWELVE

With more reports of thefts rolling in, George and I started counting the herd more often. He'd been kind enough to take it all upon himself today to give Jo and me a rare lazy morning. Besides Christmas Day, life kept me too busy to lie in bed with Jo in my arms long past time the rooster crowed, but I was beginning to feel we should partake in the indulgence more often.

After taking our time getting up, we teased one another with stolen kisses as we made breakfast. I jumped on the opportunity to feel Jo warm and wet around my fingers one more time before starting our day. So beautiful, the sound of my name in that breathy exhale at the peak of her release, like a prayer relieving me of every sin before ascending to heaven.

"That's a helluva nice way to spend a mornin'." She smiled a tired but satisfied smile as her fingers threaded through my hair.

"I wanted to make sure you knew how much I appreciated breakfast." Jo's laugh flowed like a melody, one that would be stuck in my head all day.

"In that case, I'll be makin' it every day."

That glimmer in her eye made me swoon. I kissed her again, fast, but soft and thorough. Dropping my forehead to her chest, I breathed in her sweet scent mingled with the remnants of our passions. Then, reality crept in. A groan of displeasure slipped out.

"I know," she said. "Work calls."

I nodded but said nothing. Scarce was a day when my drive to linger in bed eclipsed my drive to work, but good lord, it was impossibly hard to leave her all bare and flushed with hair as wild as her smile and eyes dark and full of love for me. I cursed my need to be responsible, but it was getting late, and George would be back soon. With one more kiss, we finally untangled ourselves and began cleaning up.

Since George had set off at sunrise, the knock at our front door meant he had completed his task. I rushed into the bedroom to grab my long-sleeved shirt while Jo answered the door.

"Good mornin', George."

"Good mornin', Miss Jo." His cheery voice carried throughout the house.

"Mornin', George," I said, returning with boots and hat in hand.

"Mornin', boss. Finally got a good rain, but it sure didn't cool down any."

"We sure need whatever we can get though."

"Yes, ma'am." George sniffed at the air and licked his lips as the lingering aroma of breakfast struck his nose. "Boy, somethin' sure smells good." On cue, his stomach growled.

Couldn't blame him. Jo made a mean breakfast. "Got some biscuits and bacon left over if you'd like some," I said, smiling at the way his eyes lit up.

"That's mighty kind of ya. I am pretty hungry."

"Have a seat and help yourself," Jo said, always happy to take care of our family. "Coffee?"

"Please." George removed his hat and wiped his brow with the back of his sleeve. He took a seat, and Jo pushed the butter over to him.

I sat down across from him and let George enjoy his meal before getting down to business. He probably hadn't eaten in hours.

"Mmm mmm," George groaned in pleasure at his first bite of bacon. "Mighty fine work, Miss Jo."

"Thank you, George."

After a few bites, George washed the food down with a sip of hot coffee. "We're five sheep short. We should check the fences."

"You take the south. I'll go north," I said, ignoring the weary look of concern on Jo's face.

"Be careful, you two." Jo's gaze flitted between us.

"Always," George and I replied in unison.

She gave us a cautious smile. The more news broke of crime, the more Jo worried. She wasn't the only one. We'd been doing well, but the newspapers bred fear. I needed to do something to make everyone feel safe again and soon. Starting with home.

I rose from my chair to fetch my holster. George set his plate aside and readied to go, but I stopped him with a hand to the shoulder. "Finish up. There's no rush. When you're done, we'll go."

"You sure? I don't have t—"

"George, eat, please. Gotta take care of yourself if you're gonna take care of anything else."

"You sound like a doctor," he said, chuckling and shaking his head before taking another bite of his biscuit.

I looked up to see Jo smiling at me and threw her a wink. Grabbing the new saddlebags she'd gotten me, I went to gather the rest of my things. Hopefully, the missing livestock would simply be a matter of downed fences because I was in no rush to deal with thieves.

I rode along yard after yard of perfect fence line. Nothing at all appeared out of the ordinary. Not until a small stretch along the trees on the path to the mountain trail. A cluster of hooved imprints and a poor attempt at wiping away boot prints had my blood rising to a boil. Whoever had stolen the livestock hadn't paid much attention to the dampness of the dirt from the long awaited rain, leaving deeper tracks than a branch could swipe clean. Riding further along the path, I stopped where it led down to the river bank. The mud made it impossible to descend with Clover today. I'd have to go farther up, then backtrack and try to pick up the trail on the other side.

A faint rustle of brush up ahead drew my attention. Though the disruption bordered on discreet, the size most definitely fit more than that of a small animal. My senses narrowed, absorbing every little detail as I drew my gun and readied for whatever would come jumping out. Slow pressure drew down on the trigger.

A pair of dark brown eyes grew wide with fear when they peered out and stared down my barrel. A downpour of tears burst free as a little girl fell to her knees. Incomprehensible words spewed out, but I recognized her fear and pleading for her life.

"No, no." I quickly holstered my gun and held my hands up, hoping to calm her down and get some answers. "Look. It's okay. You're safe."

Choking back a sob, head turned in submission, she risked a quick peek at me.

"It's okay." Only now did I register her appearance. A once colorful dress caked in mud. A round face and high cheekbones stained with the remnants of sand and tears. Splatters of blood across her light brown skin. Leaves and twigs stuck in long, tattered braids of black hair.

A helpless whimper and a few heavy breaths seemed to calm her.

"I won't hurt you. You understand?" I softened my tone.

My question met with silence and a blank stare before she finally nodded. The muscles corded in tension uncoiled, and she sat up a bit.

"I'm gonna get down." Slow and careful, I dismounted but didn't approach. "Are you hurt?" I pointed to the blood-stains.

She shook her head. A shaky arm motioned down at the river bed. I walked to the edge and pushed the brush aside. A small lamb was stuck in the mud below, exhausted from the struggle. Had she been trying to get it free? Did she know who had stolen them?

I walked back to Clover and grabbed my lasso. "Help?" I pointed to the lasso, then down to the lamb. She had already been down there and could easily set the rope around the animal for me to pull out.

The fear in her deep brown eyes ebbed away, replaced by a shine as she nodded with vigor and hopped to her feet. Showing her what I wanted done, I looped the rope around one of my shoulders, then across my body, and pretended to move behind and push. The girl nodded her understanding, took the lasso, and bounded easily down the bank.

Digging a leg free from the mud was no easy task, but she managed. She scurried to the rear, set her shoulder to its butt, and pushed, slipping and sliding as I nudged Clover slow and easy. The rope pulled tight, and the lamb mustered the energy to help with small jumps. Twenty minutes later, the exhausted lamb lay on its side, free of its muddy prison. The girl sat beside it, breathing just as heavy, a triumphant grin upon her thin lips.

"Thank you," I said, returning the smile. I walked to the edge and assessed my best path down, taking care not to move too fast and frighten her. Descending the muddy bank to reach them was a tenuous chore, but finally, I was kneeling by their side. I ran my fingers through the muck covered wool coat of the lamb as I stared at the young girl. "Where's your family?"

The brightness of victory dimmed from her brown eyes. She didn't reply as she looked off to the east.

"Bia'? Ape'?" I asked, hoping Shoshone was her native tongue.

Tears welled, then spilled over, leaving wet trails in their wake. Her shoulders heaved, arms crossing her chest in a protective hold. I scooted closer, placing a hand against her back, unsure whether or not the touch would be welcomed. When she glanced up at me, eyes now red and puffy, she lunged into my chest. Tiny arms wrapped around my waist and squeezed tight as she cried her heart out. I could only stroke her hair and hold her close until she finally settled down.

"Come on." I pulled myself free, stood, and held my hand out for her to take. At her questioning gaze, I nodded towards Clover and said, "Come with me. I have food." I bit into imaginary food and chewed. "And you're wet and cold." I faked a shiver. Tapping my chest, I said, "I'm Sarah." After a beat of silence, I repeated, "Sarah."

"Saw-rah," she said, low and soft, almost fearful.

I nodded with a smile. Pointing at her, I asked, "What's your name?"

"Haiwee."

"Hah-EE-wee?" I tested the syllables out. She nodded, a pleased smile spreading at my pronunciation.

Again, I offered my hand. This time, she accepted. At full height, she barely bested my belt buckle. Her body may have been tarnished, but her spirit shone bright. She glanced down at her muddy dress, and I waved her cares away.

"It's okay. I'm dirty too." My smile helped her relax. "Now go on up," I pointed to Clover, "and I'll get the lamb."

Haiwee scaled the trench wall with a skill I envied and I casually wondered how hard it would be to get back up there with livestock draped across my shoulders. Ten minutes later, I impressed myself with the ease in which I had made the climb, especially while holding onto an extra sixty or so pounds. Thank goodness he'd been too exhausted to struggle.

I tied off his front and back feet, then made a makeshift tie to hold him to the back of the saddle. The barn wasn't too far off, and he'd probably sleep anyway. I lifted Haiwee into the saddle, then settled in behind her and set off toward home.

Of all the things I could get up to, and Jo could imagine quite a few, I'd bet this one had never made her list.

# CHAPTER THIRTEEN

**Jo**

The sound of hooves sent me rushing to the door. While I was always relieved when Sarah returned home, sometimes my fear of the state she might arrive in could be overwhelming. Bullet holes, knife wounds, barbed wire accidents, and broken bones had all been a part of her history. I readied myself for any possibility but hadn't been prepared for the sight of Sarah with a young child and a lamb in tow, all covered in mud.

"Sarah?"

She only smiled and tipped her hat as she brought Clover to a halt at the porch steps. She whispered something to the little girl, who looked to be of Indian roots, then helped her down to the ground with a gentleness reserved for a special few. The girl glanced up with apprehensive dark brown eyes through black lashes. My heart melted. In an instant, I dropped to one knee and smiled softly to help put her at ease.

"Hi, Jo. Meet Haiwee." Sarah looked to the girl while pointing a finger at me and said, "Jo."

"Jo," Haiwee repeated.

"Yes, Jo. She'll help you." Sarah urged her on with a wave of her hand, a warmth in her expression I hadn't seen before. *Beautiful.*

Haiwee took cautious steps as she made her way to the porch and up to me. I reached out my hand and waited for her to take it. After a couple of glances back at Sarah, who reassured her she'd be in after caring for the lamb and Clover, Haiwee finally let me take her inside.

I set her up at the table with a glass of water and a loaf of bread with butter. Dinner wouldn't be ready for another hour, but at least she could put something in her belly. And she did. The loaf disappeared within minutes, leaving behind a sleepy, muddy child. I managed to hold back a laugh at her state. With the mission of cleaning her up, I heated some water and grabbed a cloth. We could get her a full bath later, but for now, I wanted to get her warm, dry, and clean.

Heavy-lidded eyes watched my every move. When I tried to help her out of her dress, she returned to the frightened girl she'd been when she had arrived. Haiwee recoiled with such force she nearly tumbled backward. I pulled my hands away and held them up to show I'd meant no harm. Intense fear paralyzed her small body. I stood and backed away to offer her space.

Dealing with children was one thing, but a child who didn't speak the same language was something else entirely. Not to mention whatever unknown horrors she'd been through surely had her on edge. I could send for Jade, but introducing another new face seemed like a bad idea. Instead,

I poured the water into the bowl, grabbed the cloth, and set them both on the table within her reach. I rubbed a hand over my face and down my arms in an effort to explain I only wanted her to clean up.

After a long moment, Haiwee took the cloth, dipped it into the water, and wiped down the length of one arm. A clean stripe split down the middle of her mud-stained skin. Two swaths later, she'd forgotten all about me and had set about vigorously scrubbing the blood and dirt from her skin. Clean water quickly turned dark. I filled another bowl and set it beside the first. She nodded gratefully and dipped into the clean one as I pulled the other away.

Sarah gently opened the door and shut it behind her. She kicked off her boots, smiling as she stared at the two of us. After hanging her jacket on the hook and placing her hat over top, she made her way to me with soft steps. Warm lips pressed to my temple, and I draped an arm around her waist.

"How's she doin'?" she asked in a whisper. The draft of her breath against my ear prickled my skin in that familiar, tantalizing manner.

"Well, she eats like you do."

Sarah's laugh drew Haiwee's attention. Sarah waved at the little girl who seemed to preen under her attention. Was there anyone Sarah couldn't charm?

"I think you have a new admirer," I said, loving the soft pink tinge my words brought to Sarah's cheeks.

No retort came, but Sarah shyly slipped away into our bedroom. She returned a minute later with one of her sleep shirts, a needle, and some thread. She dropped to a knee beside Haiwee and whispered to her.

Holding up the shirt, the young girl pulled her tattered dress up over her head. Sarah moved quickly to get her situated in clean cotton that puddled on the floor beneath her. With a gentle touch, Sarah had Haiwee standing to measure the bottom hem of the shirt.

"Jo, could you give us a hand?" Sarah asked.

"Only if it's okay with Haiwee."

Sarah whispered into the girl's ear. With a cautious smile, she nodded. I took care to move slowly, and dropped to a knee on the opposite side. Working together, we quickly had the shirt pinned up enough to allow Haiwee something to wear for the night. Tomorrow I could wash her dress and see about getting her some new clothes.

Haiwee offered me a shy smile, and I noticed a few missed smudges. I dipped the cloth, held it up, then motioned to her face, and awaited permission to touch. With a nod, she closed her eyes, and I wiped away the remaining remnants of a difficult day.

"There. All clean." I dropped the cloth into the bowl, the dirt seeping out to further discolor the water. The look of pure appreciation I received in return left a warmth swirling inside and evoked a surge of protectiveness. Whatever she had been through, I never wanted her to suffer like that again.

"Aishen," Haiwee said low and soft, eyes cast downward as her fingers tested the feel of the new fabric.

A tender smile held Sarah's lips. "You're welcome." When Haiwee's eyes met hers, Sarah brought a hand to her mouth. "Eat?"

Despite having devoured the bread, Haiwee nodded with enthusiasm. Sarah helped her back into the chair, and scooted the girl up to the table.

Her hand brushed across Haiwee's shoulder and was rewarded with an expression of pure gratitude, one that turned to me soon after. I smiled in return and offered my hand, palm up. She accepted, and I clasped my other hand on top, then tipped my head, hoping she'd understand I only wanted to help.

Sarah filled a glass of water and drank it down. When her thirst had been quenched, she cleaned the dirty bowl and tossed the cloth with the dress. She stopped to stir the stew. Pausing for a quick taste, Sarah groaned her approval. She looked back at us and gave a thumbs up. Haiwee grinned and mimicked the gesture. The pair would be locked at the hip, I could tell already.

Sarah slipped around behind me and nuzzled into my neck. Her arms slid around to lock across my stomach. "Thank you, Jo." She kissed my cheek.

My palm flattened against the side of her face, and I pressed her closer. "You're welcome."

Haiwee's watchful eyes studied our every move. A sadness swam in the depths of deep brown, though she fought to keep her expression light.

When the girl's gaze drifted away, I craned my neck to peck Sarah's lips before whispering, "Care to explain?"

The attempt at making Haiwee comfortable in the spare room had been a waste. After a half-hour of sitting with her and tucking her in, she chased after us when we made to leave. Her small body trembled in fear at the prospect of being left alone. Couldn't blame her. The poor girl's world had been turned upside down.

I shared a look with Sarah, words unnecessary. Taking Haiwee's hand in my own, I led the three of us into our bedroom. Space was scarce for three people in our bed, especially with a little girl curled tight into a protective ball. Feeling her rigid muscles relax as she finally fell asleep between us made it worth the discomfort.

I rolled onto my side, scooting more toward the middle, pushing Haiwee closer to Sarah to keep myself from falling off in the middle of the night. Hopefully, Haiwee wasn't a restless sleeper. I wasn't in the mood to get kicked or deal with a grumpy, sleepy Sarah in the morning.

Fingers threaded a soothing trail through my hair, drawing my eyes up to Sarah's. She smiled in that way that made my insides flutter. Her eyes, lit by tiny shapes of moon's rays trickling into the room, darted down to Haiwee, then back up at me.

"Do you think she has any family left?" I whispered the question that had lingered in my head ever since Sarah had gotten home. A long silence fell heavy in the darkness, an unspoken truth between us neither dared to acknowledge.

"I don't know," she finally answered, followed by a drawn-out sigh. "But tomorrow I'll see what I can find out."

Sarah looked at the girl with a longing I couldn't pinpoint. Was she seeing herself or feeling the urge to become a parent? Maybe a bit of both? One thing was for certain, if Haiwee needed a home, she'd have one with us.

# CHAPTER FOURTEEN

**Sarah**

The next morning George beat me to the barn. Getting a little girl ready had taken longer than anticipated. Jo and I combed out her hair and fixed it back into a pair of braids. We pinned her make-shift dress up to keep her from tripping, then headed out to the barn. Jo planned to take her to Jade's for the day, but Haiwee refused to go anywhere without seeing Clover first. Understanding the pull toward horses all too well, I indulged her enthusiasm. For all I knew, she had had a horse of her own before her world had been ripped apart.

Haiwee ran ahead of me in a burst of excitement until she noticed someone new inside. She came to a quick stop, then retreated behind the safety of my legs as we approached George. I had filled him in last night when I put Clover up, but he hadn't had the chance to meet her yet.

"Who do we have here?" he cooed softly when we entered.

"This is Haiwee," I said, moving aside and urging her to the front with a hand on her shoulder. "She's the hero of the day." I smiled down at her.

"Sounds like she's a pretty special little girl then." George bent down and smiled. "I'm George."

Haiwee giggled as she tested out his name.

"I'm gonna have Sam see if we can find someone who can translate Shoshone. I know we have a few folks around with Indian blood. Maybe we can get some answers and find her family. In the meantime, me and Cody are gonna ride out and check the area where I found her."

"Good plan, Sheriff. I'll take care of things here."

"I know you will. It's a weight off my back knowin' I got you here."

"Want me to take care of her for the day?"

"Jo's gonna take her to Jade's since she's stayin' home today, but I'm sure we'll take ya up on the offer soon. No tellin' how long we'll have her. Need to get her some clothes too."

"We might have some that fit."

"That would be great. Thanks."

Haiwee had moved on from us, petting every animal she could reach through the fence. I smiled at her joy and set about getting ready to ride. When Clover was ready to go, I brought Haiwee back to the house. I gave her a pat on the back and she ran inside to Jo.

I stopped in the doorway and poked my head inside. "I'm about to head out and meet Cody."

Jo dropped what she was doing and came to send me off. "I know I say it every time, but please be careful."

"I will." I looped my arms around her waist and held her close. I hoped a smile would offer some reassurance, but with the uncertainty of what the day ahead held, I simply said, "I love you."

"I love you too. Come back to me, Sheriff."

"Always."

My arms fell slack and she stepped away. I wanted nothing more than to rush back to her, to spend the day on the farm with her and forget the outside world. But the outside world had a way of invading our hideaways. Taking the offensive was the only way I knew to protect our haven. Off I went, but not before turning and giving Jo one last smile. Should I ever fail in my promise to return, I wanted that to be her last memory.

"What're we lookin' for, Sheriff?"

"Anything out of the ordinary."

Cody huffed and shook his head. "Narrows it down."

I pinned the young deputy with a glare until he squirmed in his saddle.

"I'll just ride out," he thumbed over his shoulder, "over there some." He trotted away, his wide body teetering side to side.

Perfect. I needed quiet. Hard to concentrate with him on Clover's heels, breathing so loud you'd think he'd ran all the way on foot. After a good mile of silence and nothing of interest, I caught sight of what appeared to be disturbed ground not too far from the ledge of the riverbed. I pulled Clover to a stop and surveyed the surroundings. Nothing but wide open space. The trail we'd followed seemed unremarkable, and as far as my eye could see, the same could be said for up ahead.

A stiff, ungraceful dismount came after too many hours idle in the saddle. By God, I must've looked as rickety as Abe getting up from his chair. I wasn't old by any means, but my body too often reminded me of all those miles I'd logged over the years.

At the thought, a light chuckle surprised me, tumbling out at what should have been a serious moment. I paused to shake out my legs as I glanced around again, taking in the scene from the ground view. As I moved closer, the deep groove of a wagon wheel became evident. A twenty-foot section of ground had been torn up—looked as if a herd of buffalo had run through.

Cody trotted up. "Whatcha find?"

"Not sure yet," I said, circling the large area, eyes tracing back and forth across the ground for any further pieces of the puzzle.

The breeze stirred debris on the ground, grabbing my attention. Thin and light, half stuck into the dirt, the top of what looked to be a piece of fabric fluttered under the gentle tease of the wind. I kneeled over it, noting the muddy streaks ingrained across tan threads, marred with a dark stain I knew all too well—blood.

Tugging gently, only a small square came free, giving no further clue as to what it had belonged to. I skimmed the area for more, running my fingers through the dirt. Cody dismounted and scoured the opposite side as we both worked toward the middle. The arm of a child's doll. The shaft of an arrow. Indians? But they wouldn't clean up afterward. It didn't make sense.

I stood up and walked to the edge overlooking the river. Scattered remnants of wood lined the bank. Cody came up beside me and stared down the length of the fast moving waterway.

"We should follow the river and talk to the sheriff in the next town, see if anything of interest showed up there."

The unmistakable click of a drawn back hammer sent a chill down my spine. I cursed myself for letting my guard down and allowing someone to sneak up on me. Jo would not be happy.

"Hands up and turn around slowly." The cold, deadly demand came in a deep tone.

Cody's eyes were wide with fear when he looked at me. I nodded calmly and sent my hands skyward as I turned. We came face to face with three men on horseback dressed in dark blue. All guns pointed at us.

"Well, I'll be. It's that lady sheriff." The leader, perched upon a red roan Appaloosa, peered down at us. His dark, beady eyes stood out between his battered brown hat and long dark beard. He lowered his gun, but no one else moved until he waved them down. "Sorry, Sheriff. We thought you were more of them savages."

I bristled at the vile description of the Indians, but now was not the time to debate, only to play along. As I lowered my hands, I glanced down at my clothes, then over to Cody, looking him up and down.

"Have you never seen an Indian before?"

As the three men laughed, the leader said, "Yeah, but ya see, lately they've been comin' up here dressed like us, raidin' our wagons and killin' families."

"I've been hearin' similar stories."

"Yeah. They've been on the warpath." All three chuckled at his choice of words. "That's what happened here, and it's been a happenin' all round these parts."

"Did you see it?"

"Rode up on it. The family was already dead, but we caught the savages stealin' from the wagon and takin' the horses."

"Where're they now?"

"Dead. Killed 'em and sent their bodies down the river," he answered, pride puffing his chest.

The bitter taste of disgust coated my tongue, but I withheld any response. Instead, I took in the details of the bunch in hopes of finding a clue. Rough around the edges and dirty, their matching clothing resembled uniforms but gave me little else to go on. Any qualms I had with their story had no grounds for rebuttal, even if my gut told me otherwise.

"Good thing you took care of the problem then."

The leader's lip curled into a sickening grin, further fueling my doubts and sending my hair on end. I resisted reaching toward my gun.

"We all gotta work together to keep the savages in line."

"We do," I agreed "Appreciate you fellas keepin' the area safe. Guess we'll be on our way home then."

"Sure thing, Sheriff...?"

I made him wait until I was fully in the saddle before simply responding, "Sawyer." I tipped my hat, and gave Cody a nod. We turned our horses on a heel and trotted away.

"Don't look back," I said to Cody, knowing he had the same urge as me. A second glance would only fuel suspicion. We didn't need any more trouble in our town, and deep down, I knew they'd bring it with them.

"Where to now?" Cody asked.

"Home, in case they decide to follow us. Don't want them to find out we went snoopin' around anymore. Tomorrow I'll venture out some more."

Cody didn't argue, his discomfort obvious and warranted. Seemed like a good time to give the young deputy a lesson.

"Know what rule number one is, Cody?"

He shrugged, but then blurted, "Uphold the law?"

"Good guess, but no." Laws didn't do any good when your opponent didn't respect them. "Always get home alive."

"Amen to that, Sheriff," he said with a smile.

I spurred Clover to go faster. I had a promise to keep.

# CHAPTER FIFTEEN

I spared Jo the dirty details, only letting her know I planned to look into the man's claim. I hated keeping her in the dark, but she didn't need any more reasons to worry. Getting an early start, I saddled up and headed out, leaving Cody behind. There was no need put the new deputy in harm's way again so soon. This time, my trip remained free of unexpected visitors as I made my way to the town situated down-river. Even if they did confirm the dead bodies, I still didn't buy his story. He'd been far too smug. Besides, the idea of Indians carrying out such an act still didn't sit well with me, even if the newspaper had reported the same. The stories were too similar, too convenient.

The little town was as quiet as the ride over. A few people milled about the general store loading supplies into wagons, but otherwise, nothing. Stopping in front of the sheriff's office, my boots hit the ground, and I tied Clover to the rail. A young fella—clean-shaven, well-dressed in a navy suit, and absolutely not the ranching type—stepped out of the office. His smiley expression fell blank when he laid eyes on me.

I didn't like 'em. Not the way he straightened up as if he were superior to everyone and not the way his dark eyes tried to burn a hole through me. I took good note of his appearance, including the jagged scar on his left cheek, and stored it away for later. My lip curled into a sneer, and I brushed my way past him, not giving up an inch of space.

"Excuse me," he spat, mouth twisted in distaste.

I looked him up and down as I opened the door, then said, "You should be more careful where you walk." Without giving him time to respond, I shut the door behind me.

A haggard old man thin as the rail holding Clover's reins sat with legs propped up upon the desk and a dusty old hat covering his face. He didn't seem to register my presence. My back teeth grounded out my frustration, and I shook my head. How could anyone with such an important, not to mention dangerous, job be so callous and lazy? He wasn't the first sheriff I'd ever walked in on sleeping and surely wouldn't be the last. I'll have to tell Jo and Jessie to knock me silly if they ever catch me falling into that pattern.

I stepped further inside and announced my presence with a loud and stern, "Sheriff Rawls?"

The old man about fell onto the floor but caught his chair in time. He scrambled to right himself and come to his senses. "Wha—uh…whaddya want?"

He slapped his hat onto his head and stood on shaky legs, yet to even lay an eye on me. When he did finally take notice, the look of shock nearly drew a laugh out of me, but I fought to keep the steely expression that had served me well in the past. He cowered under my glare, taking an abrupt step back and stumbling over his chair.

"Er…umm…sorry. Had a long night."

"Mhm." Not an ounce of sympathy was given.

"I'm Jimbo Rawls."

His introduction lacked the confidence I'd expected from a career lawman. I'd only heard great things about him from Carter, but the man standing in front of me was not at all what I'd imagined.

"Sarah Sawyer."

"So I gathered." He snickered at the arch in my brow. "News like that travels fast. Come." He waved me in. "Sit. Tell me, what brings you to our humble little town?"

Once seated, he appeared to regain some semblance of command.

"Well…" I said, glancing around the room while moving toward the vacant chair across from him. Slowly lowering myself into the seat, I allowed him a slight reprieve from my icy demeanor with a half grin. "As you know, things have been gettin'…a little messy."

"Don't I know it?"

"You had any problems with Indians?"

"Some reports, but none here in town. Did have a couple of bodies wash up along the river. A man, woman, and a young boy. They looked like a family though, not a band of thieves. Strange thing was, they were wearing clothes like you and me, but they were definitely Indian. A witness claimed the Indians were involved in a wagon robbery and killed a family, but when we rode out, there were no bodies and no wagon. If someone was killed, they weren't from our town."

"Mine neither. None of that makes sense."

"I know, but what can I do? I got nothin' to go on. And the newspaper says there's been lots of murders, so it's hard to dispute."

Acknowledging the statement with a partial nod, I asked, "Who reported it?"

"Some stranger passing through. Dark hair, long beard, Appaloosa horse."

"Think I ran into him the other day. Seemed like a sweetheart."

Rawls' head fell back, and a rowdy laugh filled the room. "I like you, Sawyer." He settled down, leaned forward, and cupped his hands together on the desktop. "But watch out. Somethin's goin' on, and there's no tellin' where the fallout might land. Best not to let it be on you."

"Agreed. Could ya let me know if anything new comes along?"

"Sure thing."

"Thanks. I'll do the same. I appreciate your time, Sheriff."

"No problem. Wish I had more information. Been a pleasure meetin' ya." He extended his hand as he stood, and I accepted his handshake.

When I stepped outside, a tingle of warning zipped up my spine. I scanned the street before heading back to Clover. Despite his best attempt to remain hidden, I caught a glimpse of the dark eyes that had studied me on my way in, watching my every move. I didn't let on that I'd seen him as I climbed into the saddle. Oh yes, something was definitely going on. Solving this mess would require careful treading indeed.

Was it worth it? Was it anything that truly needed my intervention beyond keeping my own town safe? I wanted to say no. Willed my heart to agree. But something inside recoiled at the idea of choosing to be blind to it all. My instincts said something deeper lurked beneath the surface and like it or not, I was needed to help impart justice.

"Just had to be made of that different metal, didn't ya, Sarah?" I muttered under my breath. I spurred Clover into a faster than normal trot, anxious to put some distance between us and whatever evil lingered nearby.

When I returned to town, I stopped into the office to see how the deputies were holding up. Charlie and Ben had arrested a couple of drunks who had busted up the saloon at the edge of town, and the night watches had stopped one attempted theft out on the hilltop. None were Indians. Otherwise, all seemed quiet. Next, I needed to address whether or not Sam had found anyone who could speak Shoshone. I'd made no progress in my search for answers, just kept running in place, waiting for a break, like the poor lamb struggling in the mud. It frustrated the hell out of me.

"Never thought I'd see the day."

An unforgettably annoying voice startled me from my thoughts. I leaned back in my chair and folded my hands on my lap as I took in the sight of my old acquaintance. It had only been a couple of years, but besides the addition of a few well-worn wrinkles, Lexi Lawless looked exactly the same.

Like trouble.

"Well, this is a surprise," I said in a slow drawl.

"You know me, Sarah, never been one for obeyin' social expectations."

"Mmm. What brings you to town, Lexi?"

"Just passin' through. Wanted to see an old friend." She removed her hat and casually examined it before wiping the brim and putting it back on. "Anything wrong with that?"

"Only that you don't have any friends."

"That hurts. After all we've been through?"

"Lexi…" Her name rolled out in a growl. She sure had a way of drawing a reaction out of me.

"Okay, okay," she said, holding her hands up in an offer of truce. "But for the record, I thought we'd made progress."

A heavy sigh fell free, and I rolled my neck, enjoying the relief bestowed by the small pops and cracks. "We did, but where you go, trouble follows."

"Guess we have that in common."

She wasn't wrong, but some of us were more gifted than others. "So…?"

"Fine. I may have overheard somethin' that might interest you." She circled the room, pausing at the wanted posters. "I could go for a whiskey."

"Lexi..." So frustrating.

"I'm thirsty. It's been a long ride."

"You wanna aggravate Jo."

"I'm pretty sure the only one that gets aggravated is you. Can't say I don't enjoy that."

Very true. I couldn't even help the roll of my eyes that proved her right. Ignoring her satisfied grin, I stood from my chair, adjusted my hat, and settled my free hand on my holster.

"Fine. One drink, and you tell me why you're here."

"One drink is hardly enough to quench a parched throat."

"You seem to be handlin' it fine." Lexi feigned a pathetic cough, to which I only groaned. "We'll see if you're news warrants a refill. Deal?"

"Deal."

"Let's get this over with then." I strode past her and out the door, making her jog to catch up.

The moment we stepped through the swinging doors of Jo's saloon, all eyes fall on us. I tipped my hat and moved easily through the room with Lexi in tow. When I reached the bar, Jo approached with a single brow cocked in question.

"Look who's in town," I said, my tone exuding my lack of enthusiasm.

"Hey, Jo," Lexi tipped her hat, a salacious grin upon her lips.

"Hey." No other words followed, only a stare-down.

"Beer or whiskey?" I asked, hoping for whiskey. The drinks went quicker that way.

"Beer," Lexi answered, still holding on to that damned grin of hers.

*So painful.*

Jo set us up with two beers and hurried away without another word. Oh, how I envied her freedom. Lexi hummed her appreciation after a long sip of the beverage and I indulged in a slow draw of my own. Might make the conversation go a little smoother.

"So…?"

"Jo sure pours a great beer. I think it tastes better among friends, don't you?" She turned to me, eyes twinkling as if a punchline were on the tip of her tongue.

Lexi had gotten too comfortable. That needed to change. I met her dead on and set her straight. "Just because we settled some old debts doesn't mean I want to have you over for dinner."

"As long as we're good to share a beer, I'd call that close enough."

Damn, I couldn't argue with that rationale.

Lexi turned back to her glass and took another long sip, falling uncharacteristically silent. Finally, she cleared her throat and said, "I hear you've been askin' questions."

"Guess I've been askin' the right ones."

"Dangerous ones, from the sound of it."

"They always are."

"This one's got government hands all over it."

My grip on the glass tightened. The tension carried up my arm and reached out to every muscle in my body.

"You need to be careful, Sarah. And if it were up to me..."

Her intentionally unfinished thought left it open for my rebuttal, but I resisted the urge to tell her off. In this case, I truly did want to hear her opinion. Lexi may have been a pain in my ass, but she was no fool.

Her surprise at my silence didn't go unnoticed. She waited another breath before finishing, "I'd think real hard if this was somethin' that needed to be pursued. Especially when I've built somethin' awfully nice for myself."

Lexi's statement echoed my earlier concerns. My tendency to jump in the name of justice had gotten me into trouble more than once. Now, I had more people to think about—a whole town's worth.

"My guess," she continued, "is that they'll come a knockin' on your door soon enough if you decide to keep on it."

I nodded, understanding I didn't have much time to decide, if it wasn't already too late. "Do you need a room for the night?"

"So, I guess my tip was worthwhile after all?" She smiled wide and cocky.

I sure did miss the days of punching her in the face.

"Didn't say it was free." The smug expression drained from her face. It was my turn to smile. "But yes, I appreciate it. And I'll get you another beer."

"Why, thank ya, Sheriff."

"Don't get used to it." I slapped her on the back and gave Jo a nod.

"Never."

# CHAPTER SIXTEEN

"Sheriff Sawyer."

I looked up from the newspaper, surprised to find an old nemesis from my past life. It had been a long damn time since I'd seen the short, stocky woman with cold, dark eyes that stood firmly entrenched in my doorway. To say the air had chilled in her presence would be too kind. I'd have been happy to never see her again. Her arrival couldn't be good news.

"Been a while, Constance."

"That it has." She ambled deeper into the office, heels clomping against the old wood. Her long, dark dress swished with each step until she stopped at the edge of my desk. "This is interesting," she said, clearly staring at the badge pinned to my chest.

A laugh bubbled out, not at all fitting the tension between us. "It is." I relaxed back in my seat, allowing easier access to my guns if needed.

Her eyes followed the movement of my hands. One side of her mouth twitched. "No need for that." In one graceful spin, she sat down in the chair opposite me. "Yet," she added with a quirk of her lip.

"I'll be the one decidin' that, but I appreciate your input." Every muscle tightened in ready.

"You always were a wise ass. And what good did it ever do you?" She glanced down at her nails, inspecting them for imperfections. "Just brought one bit of trouble after another."

"You know what they say, practice makes perfect."

When she looked back up at me, her mouth twitched again. Those dark eyes gleamed at our little game of back and forth. From the way she spoke to the way she dressed, Constance still embodied the perfect image of a proper city woman. But a rattlesnake slithered underneath the façade, poised to strike when it suited her best.

"Then, I guess you might say you've reached perfection, Doc."

Lexi was right. The messenger had arrived. How appropriate for it to come in the form of Constance Arnold, opportunist extraordinaire.

"You're butting your nose into business that doesn't concern you, Sarah."

"Dead bodies and false accusations do concern me, especially when it happens on my doorstep. My job is to uphold the law. You know, that thing you've never had a moment's concern for?"

Her head fell back with a raucous laugh. "Those were the good old days, weren't they? I should thank you for getting me out of New York. The West is definitely the land of opportunity." Her laugh settled into a chuckle, then into silence as she looked me right in the eye. "Now I work for the highest law in the land."

"You can't be serious."

"Oh, it's true. They have big plans, and there's some land they need. Let's just say, it's my job to get it cleared up."

"This is about land rights?"

Wasn't it always? Land and money were the root of all evil.

"Haven't they taken enough from those people?" I made no effort to hide my disgust.

We'd slaughtered them, enslaved them, stolen from them, and cheated them. Now we painted them as murderers of families too. An exponential number of reasons existed to be ashamed of my people. When would it all stop?

"I don't ask questions, Sawyer, I just do what I'm paid to do. And what do you care about those savages anyway?"

"A shame there's so many people like you, Constance. And what I care about is the truth. They're nothin' like what you're sellin' to the public, and you know it."

"Ah, right. I'd forgotten you'd taken the righteous path after you killed three of my men back in Omaha, Doctor," she spat out the nickname with distaste.

"Still blamin' me for that, huh?" When she merely shrugged, I leaned forward, aggressively pushing my presence into her space. "Doesn't matter what you think, but for the record, my survival is different than gettin' land for the sake of havin' more land. Different than enslavin' folks because their skin is different or chasin' the natives from their lands because someone thinks they're beneath our kind. You threaten me or what I care about, and yeah, you'll get my wrath."

We stared one another down in silence.

"I'll be sure your complaint is noted," she said with little conviction, grin falling away. "You know," she started, scooting back a touch, her discomfort bringing me satisfaction. "This is bigger than us. It'll happen one way or the other. Why should I miss out on getting my cut?"

Surely she wasn't asking me for moral advice. What was her angle?

"You're the one who has to answer that. You have to live with your actions. As for me, I wouldn't help. It's not right, and that kinda thing comes back on ya."

"Maybe." She regained her confident smirk. I'd seen that look before. She knew something. The time had come for the unveiling. "But we don't all have nice little farms, profitable saloons, and a shiny badge. We have to survive how we can."

"Then how about you do your survivin' somewhere far away from my town?"

We locked in yet another dueling stare. I didn't like her knowing about my family, but I would expect nothing else from her. I held my cards close to my chest, revealing no emotion. I refused to give her the satisfaction, and her growing irritation at my defiance thrilled me.

"I go where they tell me."

"Who? Who's in charge?" Thirsty for answers, I couldn't resist her bait, even knowing better.

"You'd love me to tell you," she taunted, a sadistic gleam in her cold eyes. "Why? Will you kill them like you did O'Shea? There will just be another."

"Killin's not my goal. Maybe I can strike a deal, find somethin' else they'd rather have."

"Tell you what I'll do," she said, her grin dangerous and suspiciously all-knowing. "I'll pass it along. If there's interest, I'll set up a meet."

"Fine. In the meantime, any chance you could keep your men outta my town? I'd hate to use any more bullets."

"Can't make that promise. You know how it is when men get bored. But I'll warn them against it."

"Appreciate it."

"I aim to please."

*Ass.*

As she rose from her chair, I did the same. My height often gave me an advantage, but with Constance, it was even more prominent. I glowered down at her. She put on her usual display of aloof power, but the brief flicker in her eyes gave her away. Constance feared me. She always was a smart woman.

"I look forward to hearin' from ya," I said, giving her no reprieve from the pressure of my glare.

"No promises."

"I have no doubt you'll come through, Constance. If there was ever one thing you were good at, it was bein' a pain in my ass."

A forced grin made its way across her lips. "Just one of the things I pride myself on, Sheriff." She walked to the door and turned around. "See ya round, Sarah."

Tense muscles slowly uncoiled, though a heaviness remained in my chest. I may have just brought the war right to our town.

The moment Constance left, I headed right for the saloon, striding straight through the swinging doors and onto the stool beside Jessie and George.

"I know that look." Jessie slid her beer over to me. "I think I'll need something stronger."

"Mhm," George agreed.

Beer would help, but Jessie had guessed right. This wasn't a beer conversation. "Make it three."

Once Jessie had called our order down to Jade, she turned and focused squarely on me. "How bad?"

"Government contracts."

"Government?" The crease across Jessie's forehead deepened as her brows stitched together.

"Not surprisin'," George muttered.

"Does make sense," I agreed. The minute Constance made the reveal, the pieces fell together. A perfectly constructed plot with all the power players to make it work. The question of who I needed to get to though, still remained.

"The government not wantin' to get its hands dirty directly, hired out," he added. "They're settin' up the Indians to make it easier to take back their land. Probably for railroad or some kinda minin'. Seen enough of it in my time out there."

"How do people live with themselves?" A storm of anger brewed in Jessie's gray eyes.

George shook his head. "Always think money solves everything. Don't get ya into Heaven though."

Heaven wasn't meant for everyone anyhow. "Constance seems to be fine with it."

"Constance? Constance Arnold?" Jessie's voice rose, her brows stretching to the brim of her hat in shock.

"The one and only."

"Wow. First Lexi, then Constance. All you need now is Helen, and all of your favorites would have been by to visit. Guess you're still popular." Her comment drew a laugh from George.

"Hmph. Not the list I want to be on. Helen would sooner slit my throat than talk to me. Which is your fault, by the way."

Jessie held up her hands. "Whoa! Hey! I was drunk."

"And what did I get for helpin' you back to your room? You pushed me against the wall and kissed me when I was supposed to be on my way to her."

At that, George sat back and laughed. Glancing between the two of us, he shook his head in wonder.

"It was bad luck that she'd come lookin' for you. But you traded up...if I might say so myself," Jessie defended, half a smirk tugging proudly at the corner of her mouth.

"You may not," I said through a laugh. "I almost lost my trigger finger when she came after me with that machete. My trigger finger, George!"

He nodded along, eyes dancing with humor, lips pressed taut to suppress more laughter.

"Never get involved with a woman who loves swords, George," Jessie wisely advised.

"I'd watch out for hatchets too," he added, to which Jessie and I exchanged intrigued glances.

"Agreed. But knives, on the other hand…" I set my eyes on Jo. A ray of sunshine pushed through the gloom of a long day as she headed our way with a smile stretched from ear to ear. Her smile was everything.

"Well, hello, Sheriff." Jo threw me a wink, then greeted George and Jessie as well. "Looks like some interestin' conversation goin' on here. Care to share?"

Jessie's mouth trembled, fighting the urge to spill my secrets. By the gleam in her eye, I knew which part she would share.

I quickly blurted out, "Figured out a few things, but not sure what to do about it yet."

Jo's eyes bounced between the three of us. As usual, she sensed more to the story, but thankfully, she only said, "I know you'll figure it out."

"We can talk more at home," I said, heading off her instinct to interrogate me later on.

With a nod and a hand pressed over top of mine, she said her goodbyes and tended to other folks.

Jessie chuckled, earning an elbow to the ribs hard enough to make her grunt as her breath spilled out. I smiled at her grimace. "Jo doesn't need to hear about *all* my wild adventures."

"Sure she does. Keeps life interestin'."

"Then how about we save some for when we're old and gray? Gotta keep some surprises under my hat."

"That's no fun. I like to live in the now. Besides, I'm sure you got a few from before we met."

Diverting the topic from me, I smoothly pushed it towards George. "What about you, George? I know you've gotta have some doozies. I mean, a hatchet? Do tell."

"Yeah, George," Jessie jumped onboard. She loved wild stories.

Before he could respond, Sam slid up beside me and whispered, "We found a translator. Says she can speak Shoshone."

"Great." Finally some good news. "Where is she?"

"At the office waitin' with Ben."

"I'll be there in a few minutes. Good job."

The young man beamed at the recognition, then hurried away.

"Guess that story is gonna have to wait, but you're not off the hook." I pointed a stern finger at him.

He smiled. "Wouldn't dream of scootin' out on ya, boss."

"Ohhh, we could do it round the fire pit one night." Jessie looked giddy as a five-year-old who'd been handed a bag of sweets.

"Oh boy. She's plottin', George. We better git."

"Right behind ya, Sheriff. Sure hope we can get some answers from Haiwee," he said.

"Me too."

We finished off our drinks, then I waved Jo down and filled her in on the news. I hoped the little girl would open up to a stranger. Haiwee was brave, strong. I saw it simmering beneath the haze of fear the day I had found her, pushing its way to the front whenever challenged. This would be no different. If her story lined up with the tidbits Constance had revealed, today would be a turning point for us all.

# CHAPTER SEVENTEEN

The old woman with dark, intelligent eyes and long gray hair tied back in a loose ponytail smiled a toothless smile when she laid eyes on Haiwee. Soft-spoken words of native tongue brought about a cautious smile from the little girl. The woman, Kimama was her name, waved Haiwee closer, but she didn't move. Instead, she glanced back at me and Jo for approval. I gave her a gentle nudge and whispered it would be okay. Only then did she take small steps toward Kimama. The bottom of the dress we'd bought her dragged across the dirt as she moved. We'd have to hem it up later.

Kimama gingerly lowered her frail body into a hand-carved rocking chair and lifted Haiwee onto her lap. We remained far enough away to allow them privacy, not that we'd understand the language anyway. Haiwee finally smiled, an honest and true smile, and it did funny things to my heart. The girl had grown on me the instant I'd laid eyes on her. Unfortunately, she wasn't mine to keep. She would be better off with her tribe, if there still was one. But, if none remained, and no one had any objections, Jo and I would raise her like our own.

Knowing the pain of losing my own family, I could only imagine how it would have felt to be reunited with anyone of blood. The selfish desire to be the one to give Haiwee a good life, however, had me warring within myself over which ending I preferred.

"Sarah. Jo." Kimama waved us forward.

Jo slipped her hand into mine, and we sat down on the wooden bench across from them. Her fingers tightened their grip.

"Haiwee says she is grateful for you both." Kimama's words occasionally hitched with the inflection of her native tongue.

"We're happy to help and will for as long as she needs us," Jo said, her words echoing my thoughts.

The woman translated for Haiwee, who then smiled and scooted from her lap to give each of us a hug. With her tiny arms around my neck, a feeling deep within stirred—a longing of the hug I had needed all those years ago. I wrapped my arms tight around her waist, trying hard not to squeeze the life out of her. The burning of eager tears pricked at my eyes, but I forced them away with a steadying breath. When we pulled away from one another, I was pleased to have kept my composure. Answers still needed finding, and I needed to stay strong for all of us.

"She says," Kimama continued, chocolate brown eyes warm and appreciative of the heartfelt exchange, "her family had to leave. The men came and forced them out. Her tribe split apart in the battle. They traveled for days. They were tired. Hungry."

Her gaze fell to the floor, her smile fading fast as the setting sun. "Three men came, pointed guns. Demanded the clothing of her parents and older brother, then started shooting." She hugged Haiwee and held her in a comforting cocoon of safety.

A gasp came from Jo. Anger coiled low in my stomach. Disgusting acts of unneeded violence. Mindless killing as if Indians were inhuman. Was extinction the government's goal? The perception they'd created of the Indians made people across the West hate them, leaving them unconcerned with their fate. Everything about it was so, so very wrong.

The fact no one else cared disheartened me. Had the Civil War been enough for them? Had the freeing of slaves absolved them from caring about the fate of any other race? Life existed in a delicate balance. At either extreme, death and disorder loomed. There would never truly be peace or freedom or any of the things people preached about and prayed for when liberties were taken at the expense of another. History books were littered with examples. Without continued compassion for others, regardless of origin or beliefs, humanity could only go downhill. Why was that so hard to understand?

But I was just a rancher. What did I know?

Kimama and Haiwee conversed some more, and Kimama relayed more of Haiwee's sad history. "Her mother protected her and pushed her down onto the river bank. She ran for two days. When you found her, she had stopped for water and heard the lamb." Kimama looked from Haiwee to me and added, "She was lucky you found her. She may have ended up enslaved. Or worse."

I knew that fate all too well. Women used and abused, tortured at the whims of men. Servitude had a different meaning for us than men. I would do everything in my power to keep her safe.

"Does she have any idea where the rest of the tribe might have gone?" I asked.

Haiwee shook her head after Kimama translated. With tears in her eyes, she looked away.

The distraught look on the little girl's face settled my earlier debate. If I could find a way to bring an end to this deviousness, I would search for the rest of her family. As much as I wanted to start now, I wouldn't. Not when they could come after her tribe again. Next time, she might not be as lucky. Danger in the West was nothing new, but this was something else entirely. Purposeful and focused, all the government and businessmen had done was take, take, take. There was more than enough land for everyone to live and prosper.

"Is there anything else she can tell us?" Jo asked. "Maybe, what the men looked like? Anything at all?"

Like a trek across the Badlands in mid-summer, the wait dragged on as Kimama and Haiwee spoke. Kimama nodded here and there between exchanges. They went on and on without translation. Finally, the old woman pulled Haiwee into her arms again and pressed her close to her chest. She rocked back and forth and began to sing, or pray, I wasn't sure which, but it seemed to bring them both comfort.

When they'd finished, the old woman spoke again. "Haiwee says one of the men had dark eyes full of the venom of a rattlesnake and rode a spotted horse."

Once again, my gut instinct had been right. My suspicions confirmed, the only piece missing now was who I'd need to confront to put an end to it all.

So many thoughts twisted like a tornado through my mind—the men in blue, Constance, appaloosa man, and the fate of Haiwee's tribe, to name a few. I spread the newspaper out across my desk as if it held the answers. The headline celebrating the growth of America in the West stared up at me. The writer boasted of wealth and new opportunities that made my stomach turn. If only they'd tell the truth about the difficulties of making it in the unforgiving new land without many of the comforts they had back East. You had to struggle to construct a life out here. Success took hard work and perseverance. But the sparkling promotions of heading west were written to sound as if you'd be handed a ready-built life of easy living.

Oh well. Life was a series of adventures. The next crop of settlers would soon embark on a grand one of their own. Of course, I hoped they'd make their home somewhere other than Idaho. We'd been lucky to avoid a huge influx of new blood, but growth of our own town was as inevitable as death.

I sighed as I thumbed through the rest of the pages of *The Idaho Statesman*, skimming the bold print quickly until one small article hidden on the next to last page grabbed my attention. An opinion column by Edward S. Carlton titled "The Indefensible Slaughter of Indians Continues Without Consequence."

The article detailed the government's broken promises to the Indians, their slaughtering, stealing of their lands, and their inhuman treatment of trying to force them to abandon their culture to fit in with society's standards. Though the government had signed bills to supposedly resolve the issues, seemed they had continued under the radar, finding ways to steal more of their valuable resources in the name of prosperity for western expansion.

"Well, Mr. Carlton, you and I may need to have a little chat."

"Talkin' to yourself is a sign of insanity."

I looked up to see Jade standing in the doorway with a greasy bag in hand and a smart-ass grin upon her face. "Well, no one ever deemed me sane."

"Ya got me there, Sheriff." She laughed as she walked up to my desk. "Jo sends breakfast and her love."

Couldn't help but chuckle at the twisted up expression that followed. The urge struck to add to her discomfort. "Please tell her thank you and that I love her bunches."

"The two of you will be the death of me," she grumbled, drawing a deep laugh out of me.

"Oh, Jade, you know we both appreciate the hell out of ya."

"I do." She sat down across from me and glanced at the paper. "What's goin' on in the world today?"

"Same as every other day, but there was one interestin' article that has me thinkin' more about Haiwee's story. Not sure what I can do about it though."

"All you can do is try, right?"

"I guess. But the goal is to protect our town, not draw attention to it." Though I may have already put an X on our backs.

"Yeah, but what I've learned to be true about you, Sarah, is you protect those who can't protect themselves." She rubbed at the scar on her shoulder. "Sometimes that puts you in a spot. That's why many people stay quiet. But if anyone can make somethin' right, it's you. I believe that."

"Thank you, Jade."

"Anytime. Just save your next heart to heart for Jessie or Jo." She gave me a wink as she stood from her chair. "I'm off to get some vegetables. Any requests?"

"I'm fine with whatever you get."

"Great."

Once Jade was gone, I set pencil to paper and crafted a message to telegraph to Mr. Carlton. I needed to know what he knew, and more importantly, how willing he was to dig deeper.

# CHAPTER EIGHTEEN

Edward Carlton was definitely not the type with a background in physical labor, but also not a man of privilege. Short and scrawny. His fancy suit and tie hung far too wide and long for his frame. A well-worn Bowler's hat sat low to his brows. A pair of spectacles atop his nose, so small he had to scrunch his face each time he looked up, gave him a mousy appearance. He stood hunched at the shoulders as if to hide away in the crowd of people receiving their family at the train station. In one hand, he held a suitcase, a small satchel in the other, peering through the herd of bodies in search of me.

I remained out of sight a moment longer, watching, noting, analyzing the man I hoped would play an integral role in the plan to shed light on the Indian situation. With the blessing of those close to me, I had sent the telegram, setting my plan into action without any knowledge of Mr. Carlton's character. Edward was not at all what I had expected. While appearances weren't everything, I couldn't help the growing suspicion that he would bolt for the next train out of town rather than put himself on the firing line.

He pulled a paper from his pocket and stared down at it—probably the directions I had provided for our meet. No point in waiting any longer. I stepped into the crowd and moved with the flow until I stood right in front of him. I'd put every inch of my height to use. My most imposing stare beat down on him. The actions served two purposes. First, to see how he'd react, and second, because I did still, on occasion, enjoy being the reason for that flash of fear in a man's eyes. After all, I did have a reputation to uphold.

"Mr. Carlton." His head jerked up, and one look at me had him stumbling a half-step back. Who could resist a grin of satisfaction at that response?

"Sh—Sheriff Sawyer?" He stammered, pushing his spectacles back up his nose.

"That would be me." My right hand settled on my holster beside my gun as I waited on him to collect himself.

He hiked his satchel higher up his shoulder and extended his right hand as he said, "Edward Carlton. Pleasure to meet you." His words came out with more certainty, even if his posture still screamed "run and hide."

I stared at his hand for a long moment. When he started to pull away, I accepted the greeting with a firm grip. "Pleasure is mine. Thank you for comin'." He didn't flinch at the pressure. Maybe there was hope for him yet. "Shall we?"

"Yes. Of course."

"Hungry?"

"I could eat."

He followed without another word all the way to Jo's, where I'd had her save me a spot in a quiet corner. Thankfully, they were in between the busy hours, making it easier to talk. Jade headed right for us, looking Edward up and down with her usual scrutiny. At least he'd been too busy getting settled to notice. She arched a brow at me, most likely asking herself the same questions regarding his fortitude. I gave her a subtle shrug. We'd know soon enough.

Once Jade left to grab our food and drink, I leaned forward, elbows on the table, and looked Edward Carlton in the eye. "Mr. Carlton—"

"Edward, please."

"Okay, Edward. As I mentioned in my telegram, I'm interested in what you know about this thing goin' on with the Indians. I plan to try and put a stop to it, and I need your help."

"How? I'm just a writer."

"As a writer, surely you understand that words are power. And I heard you also have a little pull with the San Francisco Chronicle, which means you have reach beyond Boise."

"Well, I...I can't guarantee that...and I don't have any proof. That's not the kind of story they'll run on opinions and speculation."

"I intend to get proof, and I'll start with stirrin' up ol' Governor Moody when he comes to town next Saturday."

Being an election year, it had been no surprise when we were informed of Governor Moody's intention to visit our small town. We were a short enough ride from the larger neighboring towns to be an easy stopover, but our growth and the younger age of inhabitants made us a hot spot meant to sway voters for years to come.

And he had a lot of swayin' to do. A slick businessman with a silver tongue, Cecil Moody had made his fair share of enemies, many of whom would prefer not to see him re-elected, but he did have some powerful backers. These days it seemed that was all it took. I couldn't help but wonder if he had his hands in the plot against the Indians too.

"The Governor?"

"Yep. I'll do the diggin', but it'll be up to you to craft the words that bring attention to the cause. Can you do that?"

He paused a breath before nodding. "I can." It came out more like a question.

"Will you do that?" I asked, eyes hard on him, seeking commitment.

"I will," Edward replied, this time without hesitation.

Moody's talking points would most likely be steeped in gray areas where he would stealthily avoid making any firm commitments. My true interests lay in the time after his speech ended. Not because his usual rhetoric of "all propaganda and no bite" was old and boring, but because of the question and answer time he would allow. Boy, did I have questions, and my new friend, Mr. Carlton, would be present to write about the event. Maybe there would be enough stirred up to get this started.

Yes, next Saturday would be interesting.

At the news of the Governor's visit, a pavilion had been quickly constructed on the edge of town where he could hold his speech and be the center of attention. All those political types enjoyed that stroke of the ego. With Moody's reputation, I had directed the deputies to maintain certain posts to help keep the area safe. The Governor would have his own people, but their only concern would be in protecting him. He was low on my list of people to tend to should guns go blazing.

The turnout was greater than I'd expected. Then again, no prominent public figure had visited our quiet town in many years. The Governor arrived by banner-covered train, then rode to the pavilion in a parade of those fancy three wheeled automobiles to be sure his presence did not go unnoticed. I kept a close eye on the faces, memorizing the strangers and searching out any suspicious familiars from the other towns I'd visited.

Once Moody opened his mouth, he droned on and on, delighting whenever the crowd would reward him with applause. When his speech came to an end, they had barely issued a call for questions before a man threw up his hand. Moody smiled, looking far too confident considering he had no idea what would come next. The question, too easy and generic, made it obvious the man had been a paid participant.

Enough of that garbage. I strode toward the front and raised my hand. A hint of discomfort wavered his grin at the sight of me. I'd soften him up first by playing to his ego.

"Governor, thank you for payin' our humble town a visit."

"It's a pleasure to visit the many men and women contributing to the growth and development of our fine state."

Ah, the perfect lead in. "On that topic, what's your position on the stealin' of Indian lands in Idaho, and across the West, by the government in the name of growth and development?"

Murmurs spread throughout the crowd. Moody's eye twitched, but he suppressed any outward display of emotion. He stood taller as he walked toward my end of the stage, his left hand propped in his vest pocket like the uppity man of wealth he was. His towering stature looming over me had been meant to intimidate, but I only bowed up more, staring him right in the eye.

"I have no knowledge of such actions. I'm sure the leaders of this great country have everyone's best interests at heart. They have agreements with the tribes, and I am certain they are taking steps necessary to make westward expansion a success accordingly," he answered with pride but drew none of the applause he sought.

"By chasin' them from their lands and stealin' it from under their noses?" I pressed, holding my tone even and absent of accusation.

"That's hearsay," he spat, revealing a chink in his prideful demeanor. "I've seen no proof of these things."

"What about the increasin' number of railroads runnin' through Indian lands or the gold mines in Fort Belknap?" I tossed out a few facts Edward had shared with me.

Silence came as his response. Rage festered under his skin, threatening to erupt from his bulging eyes.

In the absence of his response, I continued, "I do believe that Pledge you so proudly like referrin' to ends with '…and justice for all.' If you truly believe that, then how can you sit here and tell me that justice applies to all people except the ones that are truly native to our land? The ones we made promises to?"

"Now hold on—"

"How, Governor Moody, can you tell me it's okay that the people who owned these lands, farmed them, raised families here, have it all taken and their families slaughtered by our kind? And why? Because their culture and language don't conform to our standards or because we consider them not as smart? Kill the Indian, save the man, isn't that what they say? But they wouldn't break."

"Miss Sawyer—"

"Sheriff Sawyer," I gritted out, interrupting him once again. "And I'm not finished. Our country fought a war over the mistreatment of an entire race for similar reasons. Yet, it's okay to continue to steal and kill and manipulate another? Was nothing learned? It's disgustin', and everyone involved should be ashamed."

Jeers and mutterings of support sprung from the crowd. Moody's puffy face burned red. His eyes ached to throw daggers but were forced to remain sheathed in the company of the public.

"May I speak now?" he asked, maintaining a calm, collected tone despite the anger in his eyes.

I looked around and basked in the slack jawed men who were unaccustomed to such tongue lashings from women. They should count their blessings words had been my only weapon of choice.

"Yes," I said, chin held high as I settled my hands on my holster in a show of strength.

"Thank you. Let me assure you that the concerns of you and your town have been heard and that I do not condone these actions you've alleged. I shall assign people to look into it immediately."

*Liar.*

His answer drew a splattering of hesitant applause. Guess I wasn't the only non-believer in the crowd.

"Is there anything else I can do for you, Sheriff Sawyer?"

"Just do what you promised."

"I am a man of my word." He glowered but forced a slimy smile before putting on his politician face once again. "Thank you all for coming. I assure you I will work to resolve whatever treachery is being done. As you mentioned, Sheriff Sawyer, justice for all is the motto I live by. I trust I can count on your support when election time comes."

"That all depends on you, Governor."

A silent understanding passed through our stare down before he conceded with a nod. Without even knowing, he'd played right into my hands. He turned to the crowd and waved as if nothing had happened. His departure drew the loudest applause of the night. Surely that would stroke his ego, believing it due to his performance.

As the crowd dispersed, I waved my deputies over. I scanned the sea of faces once again while I waited. A familiar set of glaring eyes grabbed my attention and pinned me down. Constance appeared none too pleased with my questions, and her presence here had me equally unhappy. I allowed no hint of fear or apology in my expression, nothing at all that would give her any ammunition against me. A man came up beside her, speaking into her ear as she continued to stare me down. She nodded, and when he pulled away, I recognized him as the fancy man with no perception of courtesy from my visit with Sheriff Rawls.

Just then, Jo reached my side. The corner of Constance's mouth curled. The miniscule movement would've been nearly imperceptible if I hadn't known her so well. My old friend, dread, fell heavy in my gut once again. Jo tugged my arm, dragging my attention from a face I'd rather forget to the one I never could.

"Hey. Everything okay?" Jo asked, looking over my shoulder into the scarce remnants of the crowd.

"Yeah. Fine. It went well."

"It did. And you were wonderful. Maybe you should run for office."

"I second that," Charlie said, stopping a few feet across from me.

"Definitely not. This is more than enough right here." I tapped my badge. Cody and Sam joined the circle, followed quickly by Ben and Edward. I couldn't wait to read his next column. "Good job tonight. Everything went smoothly. Anyone see anything I should know about?"

"Nope," all three deputies answered in unison. Edward broke out into a mischievous grin.

Curiosity got the best of me and I asked, "What's got you so happy, Mr. Carlton?"

"Did you see how red the Governor got when you corrected your title?"

Jo squeezed my forearm and smiled. I could admit it was a favorite moment of mine too. That and seeing him flounder.

"Sheriff Sarah Sawyer, as quick and deadly with words as she is with a gun," Edward said, mostly to himself. He pulled out his pad and jotted down some notes. "This is perfect. Now I can write a column that's not just my own speculation. Readers will see that others, especially someone with your reputation, recognizes the government's evil doings as well, and maybe it will open their eyes."

"Do we have to mention Sarah by name?" Jo asked. I shared her concern, but had accepted the responsibility when I had set this into motion. "We don't need any more trouble in our town than we already have. Can't you just shine the light on this injustice and hopefully pressure the government into changing its ways?"

"We will, I'm more sure of that than ever, but it will take more than just me writing about nameless commoners who disagree with policy, no offense to anyone. The people need a leader, a face to go with the revolution, so to speak. Sarah, you are that leader. Respected and feared. Smart and determined. People will give real thought to something you're passionate enough to make a stand on."

I looked to Jo, who now beamed with blinding pride as she nodded. Then, I met each man's eyes, receiving only the same approval. "And none of you have an objection about this? No one has concerns?"

Charlie spoke up, "Objections? No. Concerns? Always. But we're kinda already in it. We might as well take the battle to them. And I will stand beside you, Sheriff."

"Me too," Cody said.

"Same here," Ben and Sam replied in unison.

"And us," came a chorus of voices from behind.

Jo and I turned around and were met with four determined-looking women. Jessie, Ann, Jade, and Lexi were all steely-eyed, with deadly smiles that meant business. Well, we had a posse, at least. And more were sure to join the cause. Tomorrow I would work on that, but tonight, it was time to head home.

"Okay then. Guess that's that. Be safe gettin' home, everyone. Keep a watch out. There are some very unhappy folks right now. Understand?"

Everyone agreed, and as we parted ways, Edward mused aloud, "Sheriff Sawyer demands Governor Moody make good on his promise of justice for all. Oh, this will be good."

Ann chuckled. "I like it."

Jo snickered, and I shook my head. Lexi shot me a grin. I acknowledged her with a nod. Like her or not, she would be a valuable asset. Jade and Edward headed for the saloon. Jessie trailed behind us in silence, but I could tell she ached to get something off her chest.

"What's on your mind, Jessie? I know you're holdin' somethin' back."

She jogged up beside me with that smirk of hers. "Nothin' really. Just…it's funny how much you protested becomin' sheriff, and now you'll be the face of Indian justice."

"I know. I'm not happy about it, believe me."

"But you are proud."

I gave her a sideways glance. Carter's joke about being the savior of the West sprang to mind, and I nearly cracked a smile.

"I know damn well how much you like standin' up for the little guy." A smile curled at Jessie's lips. "Well, no one's smaller right now than them Indians. It's just gonna be a different kinda fight. Guns ain't gonna solve this one."

"I know." Guns would be much easier, but the battle was one worth fighting. "All I can hope for is to change the direction of the war."

"I'm sure you will, Doc." She slapped me on the back.

Wish I could be as sure as my old friend. With the growing number of people by my side, at least we had a chance. That was all I ever needed.

# CHAPTER NINETEEN

With Jo at the saloon waiting on a delivery, I planned to do a few things around the house before heading into town. The table leg needed fixing from its wiggling, the front porch step had a creak that made me cringe every time I stepped on it, and the back door hinge was coming loose. Those little things needed attention before they became big things. Nothing good ever came from procrastination. They were far from the most important things niggling my mind, but fixing them gave me some semblance of control.

In confronting Moody, I'd invited the devils dancing in the darkness to our quiet town to try to silence us. As sheriff, I was supposed to protect the people, not paint targets on their backs. Hell, most people had no idea what even happened in the world outside of town.

I looked out the window, and I could practically see the ominous clouds approaching in the distance. Who would come, and how many? Would I be able to stop them?

I moved the bowl of apples to a nearby chair, then flipped the table over. Hammer and nails in hand, I stared long and hard while I worked out a plan of repair. I decided on strengthening the leg by angling a nail in each direction into the wood until it was secure. Probably not the best way to do it, but I was no carpenter. No patience for all that. The nicest piece I'd ever made was the porch swing, but it was nothing fancy. I was all about function.

I set the table back on its legs and gave it a push. Strong as an oak. Satisfied with my work and having completed task number one, I set the bowl back but grabbed one apple for myself. If only solving my other problems were as easy.

The crunch of the apple brought a burst of sweetness to my tongue, and while satisfying, would never rank higher than my second favorite flavor. Daydreaming about my first always proved to be a lovely distraction from my worries. Jo never strayed far from my thoughts.

Next, the back door. I shoved a handful of nails into my pocket with my free hand, then grabbed the hammer. As I reached for the doorknob, three knocks wrung out. I nearly choked on my mouthful of apple. Eyes watering, coughs and wheezes were all I could manage as I struggled to settle the scratch in my throat.

"It's Jackie," came from the other side of the door.

I wiped my sleeve across my eyes and swallowed down the remaining bits before opening the door. "Hi," I croaked, stepping aside for her to enter. When I cleared the remnants of apple and regained the ability to speak, I realized Jackie had been holding a basket.

"You okay?" She asked, taking in my distressed appearance.

"Yeah." I waved off her concern.

"Okay, well, I brought some fresh vegetables."

"Thank you." She handed me the basket, and I set it beside the apples. Fresh picked tomatoes and summer squash would make for a nice stew. "Would you like a glass of lemonade?"

"Love one," she gushed.

Jo had gotten quite the reputation for her lemonade making skills. She'd even made a version that mixed well with whiskey that had become quite popular, especially in summer. I poured two glasses and carried them to the table. When Jackie chose a chair, I sat in the one across from her.

"How's your day been?" I asked, smiling as she savored her first sip.

"Good. Busy. Surprised to see you here. It's been a while. How are you?"

"It's been too long, Jackie, and I'm good, thanks. Tryin' to get a few things done before I head in. Hopin', there won't be anything too excitin' today."

"I hope not. I'm glad last night went off without a hitch."

"That was a pleasant surprise."

I had expected some unrest given the lack of love our town had for the Governor and the events currently ongoing around us. Now that it had passed, however, the look in Constance's eyes when she'd seen Jo worried me most. That look meant trouble.

"What do you plan to do?" Jackie dropped her eyes to her glass. Her fingertips danced along its smooth surface.

"No idea." A light chuckle fell out, but the question twisted in my gut. I truly had no clue. I hated feeling powerless.

Jackie looked up and gave me an easy smile, "You'll figure it out. You always do."

"Hmpf. Everyone keeps tellin' me that, but I think you have too much faith in me."

"Not at all. You've proven yourself time and again. Believe it or not, Sarah Sawyer, you are a light in the darkness. Everyone sees it."

"I don't know about that. I've done my share of bad." I'd spent years enveloped in pitch black, yearning to be the darkness for a special few.

"Regardless, it's true." She shifted her gaze over my shoulder, and the happiness in her expression faded. "I wish I could shine even half as bright as you. You're like a full moon on a clear night when someone's scared to death of the dark, making the night seem as clear as day."

Silence loomed between us. Where had these thoughts come from? Couldn't she see her own worth? I refused to look away, keeping a steady eye on her until she met my stare.

"Jackie, listen to me. You shine. You shine like crazy for so many. Especially for Jessie, me, Jo, Jade, and the rest of our family. Those are the houses that count most." When she tried to look away, eyes glassy, I pressed on, "I appreciate that people look up to me, proud that I can be the light for someone in need, but you know what?" I paused, waiting until she asked me the answer. The wait took longer than expected.

"What?" she finally inquired, her words nearly a whisper. A shy smile tugged at her lips.

"The world would be much better off if more houses learned to provide their own light rather than relying on the moonlight. Full moon only lasts a few nights a month, even then, it can be hidden by the clouds. And then what?"

She shrugged and muttered, "I guess."

Her response wasn't good enough for me. Wanting her to feel it, to say it with conviction, I continued, "The more people have love and light and somethin' to live for, the less they have to look outward, and there's power in that." I stood from my chair, the action grabbing her full attention as I slid into the one right beside her.

"Some people feel love means weakness and loss. That's how I felt after my folks were killed. And then I met Jo. She was the light I needed. Through her I found my own and the strength to be more. It's contagious like that, but sometimes…sometimes things seem so dark in the world and that's all we zero in on—war, slavery, Indians, illness, drought—but there's so much more good out there if you can keep the light burnin'. Like you."

"I never done nothin' special."

"No?" She shook her head, and I smiled at the memory of our first meeting. "I seem to remember a young woman openly defying her mother's wishes of stayin' away from the saloon and acceptin' the advances of an unsavory, drunk stranger." That earned me a smile.

"That was an act of rebellion," she argued.

"Perhaps, but there was a fire burnin' in your eyes to be more, to do more than that town and your family allowed. And then you took care of me, for no reason, no expected gain, out of the goodness of your heart. I'm willin' to bet I wasn't the first person you'd acted so selflessly for, same as I know I wasn't the last. Mrs. Nash goes on and on about your visits to read to her. How many other people take the time to do that for an old, blind widow?"

"Not enough."

"Exactly. Not even me, but see? Everyone's opportunity to shine is different but no less important. Every little act can make the world of difference, and they build on one another. Don't even get me started on Jessie." She chuckled at that, and a feeling of lightness replaced the gloom that had weighed heavy over us.

"You sure have a way with words, Sheriff."

"Blame Jo." A few more beats of lighthearted silence followed as we sipped our lemonade. "Are you feelin' better?"

"Yes. Sorry. I don't know what stirred all that up. Guess I've been wishin' I could do more, ya know? You and Jessie and Jo have done so much th—"

"It's not a competition, Jackie. We're all doin' what we can, what we're good at, and sometimes, what we have to, like it or not. You're doin' plenty. I promise."

"Thank you. That means a lot comin' from you."

I leaned in close and whispered, "Can I tell you a little secret?" Her lips curling into a conspiratorial grin, she nodded and I said, "Seein' you happy every day shines brighter than the sun for me. And with how happy you make Jessie, well, even if you weren't out doin' saintly acts for little old ladies, you're spreadin' plenty of light."

A rosy dusting spread across Jackie's cheeks. I leaned back in my chair, content that I had done my job of soothing her worries. I reached for my drink, taking a sip as Jackie finished the rest of hers.

"I should be lettin' you get back to work." Jackie stood up and headed for the door.

One look at the clock said our little heart to heart had lasted longer than expected. I wouldn't be getting the door or the step fixed today, but this work felt more rewarding. I followed her to the back door and pulled it open.

"Thank you for the vegetables, Jackie."

"Thank you for the talk and the lemonade."

"You know me, full of words." A laugh, loud and free, flowed from her, the kind that you couldn't help but smile over.

"Yes indeed. Sarah Sawyer, poet and orator extraordinaire," she proclaimed with arms wide, announcing it to the world.

"Now that's just crazy talk," I said through a chuckle. "I save the fancy words for the people I care about."

"Be careful, Sarah. The people you care about worry about you."

"I know."

"Good. Now go, be that light for those who have none."

"Yes, ma'am." I gave her a little salute and a wide smile.

Once she'd ridden off, I shut the door and leaned back against solid wood. Being careful was getting harder and harder the deeper I got myself into the fight. I'd gone too far to turn back now, having called out the Governor in public, and soon, Edward would publish his column.

Sure hoped being a light for others didn't end in extinguishing my own.

# CHAPTER TWENTY

Remarkably, things had been pretty quiet the last few days. I recognized some of that light Jackie had been talking about in the way the people looked at me as they passed. They carried themselves with a level of pride now I hadn't recalled seeing before. I liked it, to be honest. Everyone should have that sense of power about themselves, but they also had to be careful about how they expressed that power. There was a time and a place. We had a good number of folks who could wield a sharp tongue but were useless with a weapon. That could be a deadly combination in the presence of the wrong people.

Edward finished his story and sent it by courier to Boise for printing. Since the editor promised him his first front-page placement, we were bringing him out to the ranch to treat him to one of George's famous smoked rib meals. The meat was probably near done, and my stomach growled at the thought of the fall-off-the-bone deliciousness.

I tossed the jail keys to Charlie, reminded him to keep a sharp eye out, and headed to Jo's. Despite the unsteadiness of waiting for the other boot to drop, I enjoyed a light mood, looking forward to an evening with our family and a new friend.

"Howdy, Ann." I tipped my hat, drawing a pearly white smile from her.

"Sarah." She set the glass she'd been cleaning down and rushed right over, ignoring everyone else in the packed saloon. "Wonderful to see you again. Can I get you anything?"

"Just waitin' on Jo." I glanced around, not only to lay eyes on Jo as soon as possible, but also to take note of anyone suspicious. When I came up empty on both, I turned my full attention to Ann. "How've you been?"

"Good. Helpin' out a little here and with Jade and the baby. Oh, and I've been learnin' how to grow vegetables with Jackie." Her smile stretched until it creased her eyes, showing off how much she enjoyed her new-found endeavor.

"Jack of all trades."

"Like you."

"I don't know what to do with a baby. Or with Jade," I added.

"No one knows what to do with Jade," she said with a humorous shake of her head. "But seems you're doin' all right with a little girl."

"Yeah." I rubbed at the back of my neck, trying to chase away the racing heat of the compliment. "Guess so." A smile pushed through at the thought of Haiwee. "Even if we don't speak the same language."

"That's just words. Words are meaningless most of the time." A haze fell across her eyes, and she turned away.

What sour memories had her statement rekindled?

Ann no doubt had many bad experiences to dwell upon. And she was right. So often words were spoken in insincere promises, lies, and deceit. Most of the rest usually served to merely fill the air. Actions were what mattered most. Actions said everything.

"Thank you for covering tonight," I said, hoping to break her free from the confines of her past. "Charlie will stop in to check on things, and I'll be sure to make ya a plate."

She turned back around, whatever memory clouded her mind had passed, leaving clear, bright eyes again. "I'm sure it'll be fine. You enjoy your evenin'. You deserve a night of peace."

A warm hand slid across my shoulders, drawing my attention to my left and the smiling face of Jo.

"I'm all set," Jo said, giving my shoulder a squeeze. "Thanks again, Ann."

"Anytime. Now shoo, you two," Ann said, laughing.

"I guess we're off." I grinned at Jo before turning back to Ann. "Have a nice night."

"You too."

I slid from my stool and ushered Jo toward the swinging doors, my hand perched low across her back. We smiled and nodded to all who wished us a good evening. Not that the townsfolk weren't full of joyful greetings on any other day, but they'd reached a new level of friendly as of late.

Next stop, meeting Edward at the General Store. He had insisted on bringing something to contribute to dinner. Standing outside with a bag at his feet, deep in thought, Edward's pencil moved in quick strokes across the page of the book he carried with him.

"Moment of inspiration?" Jo asked as we reached the store.

He startled, and his pencil fell to the ground. Edward stammered through a shy smile, "Y— you could, uh, say that."

Jo bent down and retrieved the pencil, checking to make sure the tip was still intact. She handed it over, smiling in that easy way she had. "It's wonderful you can just fall into the moment like that."

You'd think he'd never been in the presence of a beautiful girl the way he blushed beet red. Or maybe, like me, compliments weren't his strong suit.

"There's an art to writing," I said, letting him off the hook. "I'd imagine it's like painting. You lose yourself in it."

"It's true. Sometimes the words just come to me. An hour can pass and feels like a minute." Struck by another idea, his eyes flicked back to the paper, and his hand moved with great speed.

I'm no artist, but I had a place I loved to lose myself. My eyes drifted to Jo, and my mind carried me away to some rather inspiring moments. She caught me daydreaming and nudged me in the side. A crooked, all-knowing smile led to a raised brow, which had the effect of turning me red as a tomato. Thankfully, Edward had been preoccupied. I cleared my throat and took interest in the wagon loading up at the general store.

"Sorry to have disturbed you, Edward," Jo apologized, still wearing the proud grin from having teased me. "Keep goin'. We can wait."

"No, no. I got the gist of it down." He fumbled with the book until the band had it wrapped up tight, pencil secure to its side. He shoved it into his jacket pocket and picked up his bag. "Got a huckleberry pie. Said it was made fresh this morning."

"Great. Sarah loves pie, don't you?"

I had to bite my lip to refrain from a sly remark, but the sparkle in her eye dared me to give in. Instead, I agreed and moved us along. I was more than ready to enjoy our evening, pie, and all that came after.

The mouthwatering aroma of smoked meat permeated the air as we approached the farm. There was a special art to cooking meat in a way that had you eating until you couldn't bear to take another bite. When we reached the house, the fire was going, but George was nowhere to be found. I glanced at Jo, the uncomfortable itch of warning bells slithering like a copperhead under my skin. One look from her said the concern was mutual.

I climbed down from the wagon, Edward close behind, yammering on about where to put the pie. Jo followed, eyes searching the property.

"Just go inside and put the pie on the table. We'll be back in a minute," she said without any hint of alarm.

"Okay." He walked away, none the wiser.

Jo gave me a nod, and we headed for the barn.

*BANG!*

We both ducked as a shot rang out into the night. A quick check seemed all clear. I bolted toward the source of the sound. Jo followed right behind me, her breaths coming as fast as mine as we raced toward an unknown fate.

Another shot.

I drew my gun. A body flew at me from the right corner of the barn, hitting me in the shoulder, knocking me to the ground in a heap. On impact, my gun went skittering across the ground. I struggled to catch a breath and assess my surroundings. A kick to the gut came before I could do either.

Face-down in the sand, I prepared for another blow, but all I heard was a gurgle. I rolled over, hands ready for a fight. Instead, blood trickled from the attacker's mouth, then he crumbled to the ground. There stood Jo, fiery eyes shining in a deathly glare. Blood coated her blade all the way up to the pearl handle. She offered me her free hand and pulled me to my feet.

"You okay?" The tone of her words were colder than an Idaho winter.

"Yeah," I uttered in a breathless gasp, hands on knees. "We gotta find—" I started, but Jo had already gone, disappearing into the barn.

I sucked in a deep breath and followed, grabbing my gun along the way. The sounds of struggle gave me a surge of energy. George wrestled with one man on the ground. Jo had another against the fence. There was no time to process, only act. I ran toward George, who had lost the upper hand on his attacker. I flipped my gun around and struck the man with the butt end, then yanked him off. He wasn't out cold, but it was enough.

George gave me a nod, then I rushed toward Jo. She didn't need my help. Jo kneed the man in the groin. When he buckled, she followed with an elbow to the back of the head. A proud grin climbed up my face, but another gunshot wiped it away.

I swung around and found George, his six-shooter smoking at the barrel. The man I'd hit stumbled backward, gun falling from his hand and blood dripping from his chest. Sadness pooled in George's eyes. I had no idea if he'd ever killed a man before, but most people found it hard to reconcile, even in defense of their own life.

That was two dead. I spun on a heel, anxious to help Jo subdue the last man and try to get some answers. We wouldn't be getting them from him though.

The last of the attackers lay face-down in a pool of blood, throat slit. Jo sat back on her haunches and wiped her brow. A cut on her forehead marred her skin, and she was covered in dirt, but otherwise, she seemed fine. She looked up at me with satisfaction and relief, though anger still rippled through every muscle, burned like a bonfire in her eyes.

"I'm sure you probably wanted to question him, but no one comes onto our farm, attacks us, and leaves alive." Her icy expression resembled one I'd worn myself too many times. "No way."

I understood exactly where she stood and agreed wholeheartedly, even if I had hoped to question him. I slipped my gun into its holster and helped her to her feet. Coming down from the excitement, the soreness in my right shoulder made itself known. I'd taken quite the hit.

Rolling my neck side to side, I took in the bloody scene. Only then did I realize how they were dressed—each one clothed in Indian attire, but clearly not of native blood. Seeing the treachery in the flesh made me hotter than when I'd been merely entertaining a theory. It was truly vile, and I yearned to kill them a second time.

George moved to my side, staring down at Jo's kill, then gave us both a nod.

"You all right?" I asked, relieved, but also impressed he'd held them off.

"Yeah." He removed his hat and dragged his arm across his brow. "Just a little nicked up."

"What happened?" I looked at the mess made of the barn from the fight.

"The horses got rowdy, so I went in to check on 'em. There was an Indian riflin' through our tools. When I yelled at him, I realized he wasn't no Indian. Another one jumped me from behind. I was able to knock him a bit woozy and then went for the other guy. He was a tuff 'un though. He got me on the ground." George paused and shook his head. "Then you showed up. Didn't know there was a third one." He looked back at the man he'd shot, worry etching its way across his brow.

"Don't worry, it was self-defense. I'll take care of it." I patted him on the back. "You did good, George."

"Better than good," Jo added with an easy smile as if she hadn't sliced a man's throat open seconds ago.

Her lack of care seemed to throw George, but he tipped his head and said, "Thank ya. I better go check the meat."

"I can take care of that if you want to go home," Jo offered.

"No, ma'am. I've been smellin' it all day and can't wait to sink my teeth into them ribs." Gone was any sign of distress, replaced instead with his trademark mile-wide smile. "Besides, Nellie will be here soon with the kids. I'll clean up at the trough."

"Nonsense," Jo and I both protested.

"Go on up to the house and clean up," I said. George was family and no family of ours would be washing with the livestock. "There's some antiseptic on the counter in the bedroom. Take one of my shirts. But not the blue one." Definitely not the blue one.

"You don't have to do that."

"George…" I narrowed my eyes, and he smiled.

"Yes, ma'am."

"Good. We'll take care of things out here." George took one last look around before heading to the house. That's when I remembered Edward. "George," I called out. "Check on Edward. He should be in the house."

The poor guy probably hid in the closet at the first gunshot. He might've been brave with the pen, but real confrontation was another matter.

"Whatcha wanna do with 'em?" Jo asked as she stared down at the body.

I shrugged, then dropped to a knee beside her kill and searched him for clues. Nothing. On to the second. No luck. The third one, however, who looked a bit familiar, had a piece of paper with one word: *Porter*.

Not so random after all.

Damn Constance! I knew she'd be up to something.

"They shoulda done a better job of scoutin', or they'd have known I wasn't here yet." Anger rang heavy in her tone, well deserved.

"Or maybe that was the point. They didn't want you. They were sendin' a message that they could destroy what we've built."

"Maybe we should warn Ann."

I weighed our options, then responded, "They've been keepin' to the outskirts where no one can catch on to their charade. We got three deputies on watch. She'll be fine. And like George said, no way I'm missin' out on them ribs. I won't give them the satisfaction."

Jo laughed and clapped the dust from her hands. "Well then," she wiped her brow, leaving a bloody smear across the back of her arm. "Let's move 'em out of sight and get cleaned up for dinner. Guess we'll have to have a family chat about where to go from here."

"Agreed." I took the arms of the first body, Jo took the legs.

Funny how it didn't bother either of us. Or maybe it was sad that we were both so unaffected by death. Something in Jo's eyes had me wondering if we shared the same thought.

Jo and I worked smoothly and silently to pile them in the back of the wagon. We covered them with a blanket, then put the horses up. Before we made our way to the house, I had one more check to make. I whistled, and within seconds, Clover appeared at the fence, whinnying and angling for a treat. Relieved that she'd gone unharmed, a smile erased the hardened lines from a rough night.

"Hey girl. Glad you're okay." Her nose went right for my hand. "Sorry, I don't have anything." She abandoned me and stretched to reach for the tall grass on our side of the fence. "Wait." I bent down and snapped off a handful that had loomed out of her reach. She strained and worked her lips for anything she could get.

"Hold on," I grumbled at her impatience. Jo laughed at us and stroked Clover's neck as I held the treat out for her to eat. She wasted no time devouring the grass, then searched my pockets for more. "That's all for now. I promise tomorrow I'll come more prepared." I kissed her on the nose. She sniffed and huffed, then gave me a playful shove. "Love you too."

She shoved me again as if to say, "you better bring me treats," then moseyed on her way toward the rest of the horses. Left to ourselves and the quiet of nature, Jo and I stared at one another. A dusting of anger still clouded her eyes. Understanding how hard it could be to regain control, I took her hand in mine and ran soft circles across the top with my thumb, hoping to ground her the same way she did me.

"Are you okay?" I asked, reaching up to wipe at the thin trail of blood that had crusted over on her forehead.

Jo glanced at the barn, then back at me as she sighed and nodded. "I shouldn't have…"

"It's okay. You know I won't think differently of you for protecting what's ours."

"What about George?" She looked at the house. Two silhouettes moved in the front window.

"He won't ever cross you, that's for sure." That earned a laugh, and I felt a little lighter. "He'll be okay."

"It's different, ya know? This time."

"What?"

"Killin'."

"Why?"

"I...I don't know. I felt such rage seein' them here, in our quiet haven, violatin' our home. Different than bein' hunted by my family. I guess maybe, with my family, there had been a reason, an inevitable conclusion, but strangers comin' for us to hide their wrongdoin'...I felt protective in a way I can't even describe. I refuse to watch any of them walk out of jail because they have powerful friends. If they want to come for me, for us, they better be prepared to lose their life."

"If anyone can understand how you're feelin', it's me." I squeezed her hand and moved to catch her gaze. The last of the coldness dissipated from her hazel eyes, leaving only the warmth I'd grown accustomed to seeing.

"I'm pretty sure your message will be received. Let's keep George's name out of it. I don't want trouble for him or his family. Best if he's just a worker here, far as they're concerned."

"I agree." Jo leaned in and pressed a kiss to my cheek. "I don't know about you, but I'm starvin'."

"Me too." I rolled my right shoulder to work out the stiffness, which drew a questioning look from Jo. "I forgot how much fightin' hurts."

"Aww, it's cause you're gettin' old." She gave me a playful nudge.

Unfortunately, it was true, but I feigned a look of hurt and protested anyway, "Hey!"

Jo chuckled as she slipped her hand into mine. "I'd rather do other things than fight anyhow."

"Same here," I said, pressing a kiss to the side of her head as she leaned into me.

As we headed for the house, hand in hand, the rest of the gang arrived. Haiwee waved and called out to us as Jade's wagon came to a stop. Thank goodness she hadn't been here. I swooped her up when she rushed toward me. We could deal with the fallout from this later, but tonight was all about family.

# CHAPTER TWENTY-ONE

Dinner had been wonderful. Delicious food. Great company. Perfect weather. Not even the darkness of the minutes leading up could stifle the joy of having a family gathering. Haiwee played with George's kids. Jade and Nick held their baby boy on their lap. All the couples sided up to one another as we indulged in too many plates of George's expertly prepared meat around the fire pit. When the discussion of the attack eventually came up, we filled them in on the events and expressed our concerns. Everyone agreed to be more vigilant, but no one seemed afraid. I loved the determination and strength of our family. Anyone would have a tough row to hoe trying to break us.

And then there was pie and smiles and laughter and later, Jo beneath me in the way I loved most. Not many would understand the way we could process the events and carry on. Then again, not many had been through the things we had and lived to enjoy another day.

The ride in early the next morning was quiet. I wanted to slip into town with as few eyes around as possible. Edward squirmed in his seat and repeatedly glanced over his shoulder to the covered bodies in the back of the wagon. Jo ignored him, her expression stoic as ever, only softening when she'd glance at me and Clover riding alongside.

Jessie met us at the jail, along with Charlie, Cody, and surprisingly, Lexi. The wagon had barely stopped before Edward jumped out and put a good twenty feet between himself and the bodies.

"Heard there was some trouble last night," Charlie said, poking his head over the side of the wagon.

"Nothin' we couldn't handle," Jo answered, emotionless and cold. She climbed down from her seat and moved to my side.

*Damn, I love that woman.*

Charlie and Cody exchanged glances. Jessie's brow rose at the unfamiliar frigid tone. Lexi laughed. I couldn't suppress a grin. When Jo gave me a questioning look, I just shrugged. She didn't seem satisfied, but let it pass.

"Any idea who they are?" Cody asked.

"The big guy looks like one of the men we ran into that day we were out scoutin'." I slid from the saddle and tied Clover to the rail. It had taken me a while to remember where I'd seen him, but on the ride in, it hit me.

Cody hopped up in back and uncovered the bodies. "Yep. Does look like 'em."

"Let's get the photographer here to take a picture. I want proof they were pretendin' to be Indians. Then, let's get 'em in the ground. I doubt anyone's gonna come claim them."

Charlie took off in the direction of the photographer. Cody covered them back up and hopped down from the wagon.

"Now what?" Cody asked. "We goin' after anyone?"

"Not sure who yet." Constance was merely a cog in the wheel. I needed someone higher up. "But I know one thing. We need to find Haiwee's tribe...if any's left to find."

Lexi stepped forward. "I'll go."

While I couldn't deny Lexi had been helpful, I still didn't trust her. Probably never would. She held up her hand before I could utter a protest.

"I know what you're thinkin', but don't forget, I have some Indian blood runnin' through me. What they're doin' here, they're doin' everywhere. If I can help, then that's what I wanna do."

I mulled her words and read the sincerity in her eyes. This was personal for her. "Okay then. See if you can find out where they are. Let 'em know we want to help and arrange a meetin'."

"Done."

"All right then," I turned to the rest of them. "We need more eyes around town."

"Count me in," Jessie said.

"You sure?"

"Absolutely." She held my stare without waver.

"Okay. Hang on." I walked into the office and pulled open my top drawer. I grabbed a couple of stars, then returned to the group. I handed one to Jessie and one to Lexi. "Here ya go, Deputies."

Lexi proudly fixed the star to her chest, but Jessie only stared down at hers.

"It's not as fancy as a U.S. Marshal," I said smiling, but hesitant. Was this out of a sense of obligation, or did Jessie truly want to wear a badge again?

"It's not that. I just...I was sure I'd never wear one again." She ran her fingers over the metal until a small grin took ahold of her lips. She slipped the pin through her shirt and closed the clasp.

"Looks good on ya."

"Who ever thought I'd be takin' orders from you?" She slapped me on the back, and we shared a laugh until her smile dwindled. "Jackie's not gonna be happy."

"Nope. Good luck with that." It wouldn't be easy, but Jackie would understand.

"Thanks," she grumbled, a mixture of fear and sorrow in her eyes.

Edward scribbled like crazy in his pad.

"No names." He looked up at me, confused. "Whatever you're writin'," I clarified, "no names of the deputies or anyone besides me. Got it? I want that target on me, not them."

"Understood."

"Good. So," I addressed the rest of the group, "if you know anyone willin' to join us in protectin' the town, let's get 'em here. The more help, the better. I want to keep an eye out at all times, especially on the places at the edge of town."

The cold swept in again, creeping under my skin as it tended to do whenever I felt the prickle of danger approaching. Jo pressed closer to my side, and I basked in her warmth.

"I might know someone," Charlie said. "But maybe we should have a town meetin' too."

"Good idea. And it'll be interestin' to see what happens once Edward's column runs."

All eyes turned to the writer, who froze mid-scribble and looked up at the group. Soon, the public would see the words in black and white blazed across the front page. Whether or not it garnered any support for the cause, the people involved would not be happy, but we were in too deep to turn back now.

# CHAPTER TWENTY-TWO

A few new faces appeared in town, and a few too many of them had eyes on me. I didn't like it, but for now, I could only wait. I rested my elbows on the rail and watched the morning traffic filter up and down the street. People would tip their hats or issue a good morning on their way past.

Sam rode up all fresh-faced and ready to go. "Mornin', Sheriff."

"Good mornin'. You shaved your beard?"

"Yeah, felt like time for a change."

"Looks good."

"Thanks.

"You ready?"

"Yep."

I climbed into the saddle and used the time it took me to turn Clover around to scan the streets again. One cowboy stood out. He did his best to hide behind his newspaper, but I still caught him peeking over the top. Constance had her little helpers everywhere.

As Sam and I rode out of town, I constantly checked to see if we'd been followed. About ten minutes out, two horses appeared on our trail. They didn't seem to be in any hurry to catch up, but their presence still made me suspicious.

"Looks like we have company," I said.

Sam twisted around in his saddle to get a look. "Wantin' to keep track of our visits?"

"Maybe. They were watchin' us in town too. Have you noticed anyone?"

"Can't say that I have, but I uh, hadn't been lookin'."

"You need to start," I said, hoping to stress the importance of awareness at all times. "Pay attention to the little things. Unfamiliar faces in the street. Eyes on ya when you're doin' nothin' special. See what ya see. You'd be amazed what ya notice."

"Will do, Sheriff."

An hour later, they hadn't gained much distance on us, but they were no longer my concern. The three riders who'd veered onto the trail ahead seemed far more determined in their approach. They wanted us pinned in and had executed it to perfection.

Damned Constance.

"What should we do, Sarah?"

"We're in a bad spot. We wait and see how it plays out. If they wanted us dead, we'd have seen some bullets by now."

"Hope you're right."

*Me too.*

When we were about thirty paces apart, the men came to a stop, blocking our path. Dressed in all navy blue, neat and tidy as a uniform but with no markings, they were all business. No point in trying to evade them. I settled my right hand near my gun, the left still holding the reins. Before I could ask their business, the one on the far right spoke up.

"Sheriff Sawyer, there's someone who wants to talk with you." The man, who looked not much older than me, was definitely not from the West. He sat stiff and formal in the saddle, his words precise.

"Tell Constance she should make an appointment. I have somewhere to be."

He laughed. "She figured as much."

I glanced over my shoulder. The two trailing us had made big gains and now had rifles drawn.

"She also said you'd behave if you wanted to keep your friend alive."

Of course. She always played dirty. Can't say I didn't want to hear what she had to say though.

"I do prefer my friends alive, although there's a few I could do without."

At that, he snickered. "I'll be sure to let her know."

"I'm pretty sure she already knows. Lead the way, and I'll remind her."

"There's no need for violence. She just wants to talk."

"Sure. Sounds like you know her well."

Sam chuckled, but his jovial mood sunk when a rifle cocked behind us. He turned to look. The color drained from his face at the sight of a long barrel pointed at him.

"Let's go then," I grumbled.

We rode for about a mile before they led us to a small cabin barely noticeable against the rocky terrain. One rider dismounted and ordered me to come along inside. The others led Sam away. I didn't like being separated, but it was the only way Constance could guarantee her own safety. A cowardly move, but a smart one. I tried to see where they'd taken Sam but was yanked away by the elbow. A barrel pressed uncomfortably against my ribs.

When I stepped inside the cabin, Constance was seated regally in a large red chair flanked by two men clothed all in navy, like the others. Their pose seemed out of sorts considering we were standing in a plain wooden cabin in the middle of nowhere.

Had she been anointed queen now?

"I'm flattered you needed this many bodyguards just to talk with me." I pulled my arm free from the man's hold and stepped away from the barrel. With one look from her, he relaxed and moved back to block the door.

Her eyes narrowed on me. "You always did have a big ego."

"Not big enough to get a fancy chair with royal guards though."

She sneered with disgust, eyes blazing. "You've certainly stirred up quite the hornet's nest, Sarah."

"I do my best."

"Word is you got Moody's breeches in a bind after that story. To use a saying your people are familiar with, he's been frantic as a squirrel preparing for winter trying to get his nuts sorted. Rather funny actually. These people are so much more amusing than New York City, where everyone is either more concerned with dinner parties and plays or working their fingers to the bone for pennies. There it's stuffy and dirty, and no one cares about anyone else."

"We're not here to amuse you, Constance, we're here to build a life and work together. The Indians just want to preserve their way of life. And you wanna talk familiar? The reasons people are leaving the East in droves are the same reasons you left. Only you became part of the regime that's now ruining the West too. Why? Why leave what you hate and then bring it with you?"

"It's only ever been a matter of time before the East spilled over to the West. It's inevitable. Big cities and tall buildings. No more dirt, no trees. No place for people like you."

"Maybe, but won't be in my lifetime."

"That arrogant defiance was always one of my favorite things about you." She lifted a bottle of whisky and held it up, casually inspecting the amber liquid inside, then set it down. "How's Jo? I heard there was some trouble at the ranch."

The fake smile she put on had me itching to wipe it from her face, but her words had me on the verge of actions that would not end well for either of us. Or Sam. I swallowed down my anger and fought to restrain any outward expression that would bring her satisfaction. The humor dancing in her eyes said I'd failed.

Might as well lay it out there then.

"She's fine, no thanks to you. I should kill you right now for that." My fingers curled into tight fists.

"I have no idea what you mean." She had never feigned ignorance well. Too smug.

"Mhm." *Take a breath, Sarah. Remember, you gotta get back to Jo.* "So what's the grand plan here? Kill every Indian?" I stepped closer, ignoring the presence of the other men in the room whose hands had moved to their guns. They might get me, but I'd get her first.

"Of course not. We're not the savages here. Only the ones who refuse to bend to our will."

"If you could only hear yourself," I spat with disgust. "Is that what the government's preachin'? I thought you were smarter than that, with all that fancy East education you got."

"Maybe that education is why I know which side I should be on."

"It's the money. You've already said as much. Not so hard to believe after you set me up for killin' Red. Stagin' murders is your specialty."

"Yes, well, we all have our talents."

"Talk to your people yet?"

"I did." Constance placed both hands on the desk and leaned forward. "Here's the deal, in two weeks this will all be over, so you mind your own business, quit stirring up trouble for me, and I quit messing with that little town you love so much…and that pretty lady of yours."

"Or?"

"Do I really have to say it?"

"There's a way to stop this, and I'll find it."

The burly man to the right drew his gun. Constance waved him down and shook her head. "No, I won't make her a martyr," she said to him, then looked back at me with an evil grin and said, "Might make you a goat though."

I didn't bite, only stared and dared her to threaten me again.

"This is bigger than you, than us. They'll get what they want, Sarah, one way or another," Constance said in a weak final attempt to sway me.

"We'll see. Where's Sam? I have things to do."

She threw a nod outside. I turned my back on her and strode for the door, ignoring her call of "see you again soon." I shot the man blocking the front door a deathly stare that earned me the flinch I'd been aiming for as he stepped aside.

These were the men she surrounded herself with? Weak, cowardly sheep that followed without question? Sad really, but made perfect sense. Who else would go along with such disgusting acts?

They were a gang, like any other, only these men were here for meager pay and not for the thrill, the riches, or the excitement of committing a crime. It was a job. They may have been acting under some secret government authority, but they were no better than the O'Shea's of the world. In fact, I would argue they were much worse. They didn't even know what they were doing, or maybe they didn't care, and that part angered me the most.

Long minutes passed before Sam was led back, positioned between four others, looking nervous and sweaty but unharmed. I released Clover's reins from the rail and climbed into the saddle. The men came to a halt and let Sam ride out to meet me. Without a word, I spurred Clover into a trot, and we headed back to town.

"What happened?" he asked.

"Just catchin' up with an old friend."

"Yeah well, next time, can we do it at a saloon or somthin'? I thought I was gonna get strung up."

"I'll be sure to send in my request, but hopefully, there won't be a next time," I said, though it was inevitable I'd see Constance again. The question was when?

The days that followed had been quieter than expected. I had fully expected more attacks from Constance, or the man in charge, but instead, it had been eerily silent in a way that sent prickles along my spine. I didn't like it. To make things worse, I felt like a lone sheep in an open field, waiting for a wolf to spring from the shadows. Vulnerable was no way to live, but in this game, I had little choice.

There hadn't been much news about the Indians. Governor Moody had given a quick quote condemning their harsh treatment, but no action had been taken as of yet. Typical. Their strategy probably ran along the lines of lay low, let the heat settle, and let people forget about it all.

No such luck in this town.

Our meeting had garnered plenty of support for the cause, and it surprised me to see how many had the courage to stand by the Indians. That our little town, even newcomers who'd traveled an ocean to make a life here, would take a stand for the rights of others made me proud. Now, we needed to find out where the next skirmish would be. I had a feeling if we found Haiwee's tribe nearby that would be the place.

Ask and you shall receive.

Lexi Lawless appeared in my door, a smug grin on her face and a flask in her hand. She tipped it back and indulged in a swallow, then closed the top and stuffed it into her back pocket.

"Guess what I found?"

When I didn't reply, she rolled her eyes and stepped further inside.

"Your Indians. I found 'em."

"Where?"

"They were not happy to see me," she answered. "Nearly got myself scalped."

"I can understand their feelin's." Like right now, for instance, ignoring my question to focus on herself, as usual.

Her lips pressed into a thin line. "I thought we were past that."

"We are, but it doesn't change the fact."

"Remind me why I put my neck out for you again?"

"Because they're your blood, and it's important to you," I reminded her of her own words.

"I wish your memory was a little more like your patience—short," Lexi said, looking pretty proud of herself.

I leaned back in my chair and let out a huff of amusement. "Where are they?"

Lexi reached into her jacket and pulled out her badge. "Other side of Arco." She pinned the star onto her vest. "What?" she asked under the pressure of my stare. "Say what ya want about me, but I ain't got a death wish."

"Fair enough." I stood up and adjusted my hat. "Are they good with a meetin'?"

"Chief agreed. He speaks pretty good, but I'd bring Kimama to make sure there's no confusion. And we gotta be careful. There's been plenty of mischief in them parts. Lots of travelers too."

"Guess we better get packed up then."

# CHAPTER TWENTY-THREE

The sun had barely cracked the horizon before I was up and ready to go. So, too, was Jo. There had been some heated discussion last night, but it seemed she'd accepted I'd be accompanying Kimama and Lexi to the tribe's camp. Apparently, though, the hours of sleep had brought about a resurgence of objection, which she began voicing again the moment my feet hit the floor.

"Why, Sarah? Why does it always have to be you? You have deputies."

"I do, but I'm the sheriff, and I'm the best one for the job."

"I know." She turned her eyes to the window. "But please, they signed up to help too."

"I'm the one who started this. Yes, they're here to help, but I'm the one who took on this fight and unlike the government, I won't send others to do the work for me. How do you think I'll feel if I sit home safe and someone else gets killed? What if they can't protect Kimama? What if they mess up the meetin'? The strongest people bear the largest responsibility. That's me, Jo. With or without the badge, it's my job."

Anger and pain roiled in Jo's glassy eyes. She took a steadying breath as she shook her head. "And how do you think I'll feel if you're the one that doesn't come home?"

"It won't be," I answered with confidence despite my own doubts.

"We all meet our end sometime, Sarah. I'm afraid that if you keep pushin' your luck it'll be sooner than later."

"Jo…"

"No, Sarah. I'm not ready to lose you yet. We're just gettin' started, and it's been such a fight to get here."

"You know my goal is to get back to you every time I leave here. You're my heart, Jo."

"Then why are you always rushin' to leave?"

Jo's words kicked like a mule to my chest. I stumbled backward and turned away to suck in a breath. I covered the hurt by grabbing my holster from the bed, then settled the leather across my hips and fastened the buckle. The weight of the guns helped to dull the ache boring its way through my insides, and I opened myself to the protective darkness within.

"I'm sorry," Jo rushed an apology. "I shouldn't have said that. Sarah, please look at me."

"It's fine," I muttered between gritted teeth before turning back around.

Jo's mouth hung open. Her next words lay frozen by whatever she saw in my eyes. Only a breath passed before she reclaimed her wits, but the sag in her shoulders said she'd recognized the distance I'd already put between us.

"Sarah, I didn't..." She exhaled a shaky breath and stepped closer. "You've more than proven yourself. I'm just mad and worried, and well, there's no good excuse. I—I never want to be the one who hurts you, but I did. I'm so sorry." The tips of her fingers stroked the back of my hand. "Truly. I love you so, so much."

Pulling my hat down tight onto my head, I forced a smile. "I love you too. Don't worry. I'll be back soon."

I leaned down and pressed a chaste kiss to Jo's lips. Her arms snaked around my neck, pulling me in close. Soft lips parted, her tongue desperately seeking my own. I allowed her to take what she wanted, but withheld the absolution she craved. As we pulled apart, the pain in Jo's eyes said it all. The cut of her words had wounded me deeper than an apology could heal in the heat of the moment. Deeper than her most passionate kiss could soothe. I needed time. I needed space. I needed answers.

Without a second glance, I walked out the door. Her boots clacked against the floor in frantic steps, following close behind, but fell silent at the porch. When I'd settled into my saddle, I gave her another look and tipped my hat.

"Sarah..."

No. There would be no more talk. I turned Clover on a heel and spurred her into a gallop, leaving Jo in a cloud of dust.

I reached Jackie and Jessie's house in record time. Jackie occupied her favorite front porch chair, a shirt across her lap, a needle and thread passing back and forth through the cotton with great skill. She looked up from her chore with a smile.

"Mornin', Sarah."

"Mornin', Jackie. It is a beautiful one."

"Sure is. The sun's been givin' us quite the show the last few days. Can't remember seein' such beautiful colors before."

"Me neither. They say it's the dust from this drought causin' it. As pretty as it is, I'd be happy to see it gone."

"Same here. That rain was a tease." She tied off her stitch, bit through the thread, then stuck the needle into the wood of her chair. "Jessie's out mendin' the fences behind the barn."

I tipped my hat and nudged Clover forward.

"Stay safe, Sarah," Jackie called out as I rode away.

A wave of my hand served as my acknowledgement. Why'd everyone act like I went looking for trouble? And speaking of trouble…

"Goin' somewhere?" Jessie asked without derailing her attention from skillfully pounding nail after nail into the boards.

"Lexi found the tribe." Jessie stopped and nodded before turning to face me. "I need you to look after things here."

"You never need to ask."

"I know."

"How long will ya be gone?"

My eyes turned toward the horizon, and I shrugged.

"What's wrong?"

"Nothin'."

"Mhm."

Steely eyes burned into me when I returned my focus to her. "Everything's fine, Jessie."

"Let me guess. Jo's not happy with you goin' out? Not that I blame her."

A streak of cold coursed through my veins. "It comes with the badge. You know that."

"I do." She set the hammer down, removed her hat, and wiped the sweat from her brow with a swipe of her arm before putting her hat back on. "But it don't make it any easier on her, especially with those greenhorns you got."

"I can't rely on others, not for this. Lexi is one thing, but she can't protect Kimama alone, and the others are too green. I can't sit home and put them at risk."

"But they are. Anyone who wears that badge is at risk. That's why I thought long and hard about puttin' it back on."

"Maybe, but they signed up because that's how the people of this town are. They'll run to slaughter without a thought for one another."

"It's brave."

"Maybe. But it's also stupid. You know it takes more than pinnin' it to your chest, and they ain't got it in them. I don't want their blood on my hands. Their sons and husbands not comin' back because Jo wants to keep me safe. I started this, and I'll take the lead till the end."

"I know." A silence stretched between us, full of understanding. "Sometimes though, that's what happens when you're the leader. You'll feel responsible whether they die under your command or not." Jessie's gaze turned to the horizon for a breath before returning to me. "Do what you have to do, Sarah. We'll take care of things here."

"Thanks, Jessie."

Those piercing eyes held mine for a long moment until she turned for her hammer again. "Take care of yourself, Sheriff."

"I will." I spun Clover around and headed out. Jessie calling out for me again brought me to a halt. When I glanced over my shoulder, I faced the most intense stare she'd ever pinned on me.

"Don't lose yourself in this hunt, Sarah. Jo's strong but…just don't."

A thickness rolled down my throat with a hard swallow. I nodded, but darkness already threatened to cloud the edges of my vision, its grip growing stronger with every step farther from home.

# CHAPTER TWENTY-FOUR

While I understood Jo's fears, the trip was of the utmost importance. We didn't have much time to act. I also didn't need one of those greenhorn deputies doing anything that might cause friction with the Indians. So, despite what I'd told Jo, it would only be the three of us making the trip. The situation was much too delicate for mistakes.

The ride out to the tribe's camp was uneventful. We stayed off the main routes, avoiding the problem areas. Lexi led the way, and I trailed at the rear. Positioning Kimama in the middle was our best bet for keeping her safe in the event of an ambush. I had no doubt the hired hands would not be kind to her, and the very thought set my blood to boil. My fingers kept a tight hold on the reins. I sat tall in the saddle, eyes continuously scanning for any signs of trouble.

Hours later, we rounded a bend, and there they were—two rows of teepees with Indians milling about in the distance. Small streams of smoke stretched from their fires to the sky. An arrow landed at the front feet of

Lexi's horse, bringing us to an abrupt halt—the warning clear. I had no doubt they could've picked us off one by one without a hitch. My first instinct was to protect Kimama. I blocked her on the side of the arrow, hoping we weren't completely surrounded.

Lexi stretched both hands high, and we did the same. Our wait was brief before five warriors riding bareback with bows and spears in hand circled us. Though the situation awakened every survival instinct inside, I also had to admire the way they worked as a perfect unit.

"We're here to see your Chief," Lexi said.

Two of them looked past her to Kimama, questions in their eyes. When Kimama spoke in their tongue, the warriors looked at one another. One nodded. Another peeled off and galloped toward camp. The rest remained, looking us over with a mix of curiosity, fear, and mistrust, though they signaled for us to put our hands down.

Couldn't fault them for that, given their situation. I kept as keen an eye on them as they did on us. Lexi also stood on high alert, sitting stiff in the saddle, ready for anything. Not another word was spoken until the warrior returned with two others. One of them looked much older, dressed in full tribal regalia, obviously someone of high stature within the tribe.

He held up his hand in greeting, then brought it to his chest and said, "Chief Running Bear."

I did just as he had, introducing the three of us. He gave us each a nod.

"Why you here?" he asked, delivering his words with authority, though stilted and laced with a hint of caution.

"To help," I said.

"Help?" He cocked his head to the side, eyes studying the three of us with the scrutiny of one who had been scorned too many times.

Kimama spoke up. The moment their native tongue reached his ears, his spine straightened, and he listened with great interest. In that moment, I wished I'd asked Kimama to teach me their language. If for no other reason than to communicate with Haiwee on her level. But I'd been too busy. Too busy for a little girl.

The realization pierced like one of their spears through my chest. How many other things had I ignored? Was that another reason to add to the list of why Jo had been so angry?

All eyes turned to me, waiting with expectation for something I apparently missed. Thankfully, Kimama repeated the question. The Chief had asked about my plan. Well, good or not, I only had one idea. Either it would work, or we would all die. As Kimama translated my words, the Chief locked his eyes on mine.

"You stand with us?" His tone reeked of disbelief, and his look of shock would have been funny if it hadn't been so sad. How lonely it must be to feel like the entire world was out to get you.

"We do," I said, my voice sure and strong, leaving no question.

His wide, dark eyes took each of us in, holding me in his sights the longest. Once satisfied, he turned to speak to his men.

"What's he sayin'?" I whispered to Kimama.

"He is seeking their council."

I tried to remain calm and confident, but I'd never felt more vulnerable. I disliked the insecure feeling immensely. A few tense minutes dragged on until the Chief finally fell silent, and six sets of eyes fell back on us.

"Come," was all he said before the Chief and two of his men spun their horses around and headed toward camp. The other three rode up the hill to resume their post.

Lexi looked at me and shrugged, but Kimama smiled and waved us forward. "This is good sign," she said and spurred her horse to follow.

When the women and children saw us, they cowered in fear, darting behind the thin veils of animal skin walls. My heart crumbled for them, but my anger found new fuel. These people deserved better, and I wanted to give it to them.

We followed the Chief's lead, dismounting our horses and following them to a large fire pit in the center of their camp. He sat down and pointed at a spot for us. Once we were all settled in, the people of the tribe slowly filtered in behind their leader, wide-eyed, and full of cautious curiosity. We were definitely an interesting mix, one that would evoke questions from any crowd.

The Chief took a heavy breath and began to speak. Unable to convey his message in English, Kimama translated, "We have suffered much loss and pain. Families torn apart, and rivers of blood spilt over land promised to us. The white man has betrayed us over and over. He only knows greed and destruction. There is no respect for land or creature. I do not know if you can help us, but the warrior spirit is strong in you, Sarah Sawyer. We would be honored to have you fight by our side."

"Thank you for your trust, Chief. I will do everything in my power to get you back to your land and put an end to this."

At the translation, murmurs spread throughout the tribe and the many sets of worried eyes turned hopeful. I warmed at the sight. I didn't want a war, we would never survive one against the government, but the Indians deserved justice. They deserved to have what they'd been promised and to have the people responsible for theft and murder held accountable. We'd set the wheel in motion, and now we'd have to see how it played out.

One more matter needed tending to before we left. I placed my hand on Kimama's and asked her to find out if Haiwee belonged to their tribe. My breath remained low in my chest, refusing to find its exit as I awaited his reply. His dark brown eyes gleamed like the lake at dawn.

I had my answer, and it hurt more than I ever imagined. Haiwee had a home, a family. She had been mourned, and now she could be returned once this ended. I promised to keep her safe until their tribe returned to their land. In return, he asked that I make sure she'd be cared for in the event they all perished. No easier request had ever been made. She already felt like family.

"When we return," I said, ice in my tone, "be ready to fight."

**Jo**

Sarah and Clover faded into a line of dust that rose against the gray and orange sky of dawn. The sun may have been rising, but my heart descended into the darkness of night. I knew we would work it out when she came home, but having her leave angry with the crushing weight of doubt in my mind was killing me. All I could think was, "what if?" What if this was the time she didn't make it back? No matter how skilled she was or how many times she had cheated death, the possibility had never been more real.

I sipped my coffee and stared at the horizon, too lost in thought to notice the sky's shift to bright blue. Constance and her band of henchman were no joke. They were the worst people—deadly and without conscience. There was no telling who else might be under her thumb. Not to mention the many desperate souls who'd taken to robbing folks along the trails. At least Sarah had help with her.

A knock on the door sent my heart into my throat. Had Sarah come back? Not likely. My cowgirl was far too stubborn. Besides, she wouldn't knock. Still, I couldn't help but feel hopeful as I rushed to find out. I yanked the door open, breathless and full of suspense, but every bit of me deflated at the sight of George and Haiwee on my doorstep.

"Mornin', Miss Jo." His bright smile fell flat as he took in the sight of me. "You okay?"

"Ummmm…yeah." I let out a shaky breath and smoothed my hand across my hair. "I'm fine, George. Good mornin'."

Forcing an exaggerated smile, I knelt and gave Haiwee a hug. She looked adorable in the little blue bloomers Nellie had given her. "Mornin'," I said, then kissed her on the cheek.

"Maw-nin', Jo," she said, a shy smile spreading across her lips.

"You sure learn fast." She may not have understood my words, but Haiwee's rosy cheeks insinuated she knew it to be a compliment. I took her hand in mine and stood up.

"She sure does. Nellie's been tryin' to get her some basics." George let out a short chuckle. "Before too long, she'll probably be talkin' our ears off."

"No doubt." I stepped aside. "Come on in." I led Haiwee to the table and pointed to the eggs. She agreed with enthusiasm. The little girl sure could eat.

George picked a small sack up off the floor and carried it in, still keeping a careful eye on me. "You sure you're okay? You look upset."

"Eh, Sarah and I had a disagreement," I answered. No point in hiding it from him. "Won't be the last one. She's stubborn as a mountain goat sometimes."

"She is," he said, nodding as he set the sack on the table. "So are you, if ya pardon my sayin' so."

I rolled my eyes and couldn't help but laugh as I cracked one egg into the skillet. "I know. I just wish she'd be more reasonable sometimes. Yes, I know she can take care of herself," I rambled, no stopping it now. "But things are escalatin'. You can't have too much help right now, yet she insists on puttin' herself in the crosshairs more than necessary." With the egg well underway, I took a deep breath to gather myself. "Sorry, George."

"Don't need to apologize to me. I asked."

His easy going demeanor was refreshing. I gave him a smile, then cast a glance at Haiwee, who watched me with concern in her eyes. Again, I gave her a smile, but this one came a little easier. Seemed I'd needed to get that off my chest.

"Thanks for listenin'."

"Anytime. But for what it's worth, I'm sure Sarah won't go doin' nothin' that ain't necessary. And she darned sure ain't goin' off half-cocked. She'll be fine."

"I know." I did know, but it never quite quelled the worry that gnawed at my gut every time we were apart. "Thanks for keepin' Haiwee last night." A change of subject was needed. "I know she enjoys bein' around other children closer to her age."

"Anytime. And here's a few more bits we found that might fit her."

"Thanks so much. She loves the clothes."

He smiled and patted Haiwee on the back. "I best be gettin' to work."

"Have a good one, George."

"You too, Jo. And don't worry. You can talk it out tonight."

My lips pursed into a tight smile, guarded, but full of gratitude. Haiwee called out a goodbye and waved as George closed the door behind him. She turned her attention back to me, smile fading. Haiwee may not speak our language, but she was adept at reading our emotions. She didn't need to worry about me, but I appreciated that she cared.

"Ready?" I asked, holding up the hot skillet.

She nodded feverishly, grinning wide as she said, "Eat."

"Yes. Let's eat." I slid the egg onto a plate and set a slice of bread on top. I handed it to Haiwee, along with a fork, and watched her devour the meal.

Despite my lack of appetite, I grabbed a slice of bread, sat with her, then filled the air with unimportant chatter to distract myself until Haiwee had finished. Once she'd gotten her fill, it was time to get on with my day. Lord only knew how many hours I had to kill before I'd see Sarah again.

Twenty minutes in the garden had been enough to drive me crazy. The ever-present voice in my head cycling through every detail of our fight and what I'd say when she returned only stirred the pot and made me more anxious. I'd hoped having an energetic child to entertain would have been enough to silence the chatter, but no such luck. It was going to be a long damned day.

"Want to go see Jackie?" Haiwee's eyes lit up, giving me an immediate answer.

Haiwee was an amazing little girl. She had tons of love to give, even with the horror she'd seen. Maybe because she'd been lucky enough to be found by Sarah instead of one of the many other tragic what-could-have-beens. Now Haiwee had the chance to see that not everyone treated her kind with hatred and disrespect, even if the color of our skin was the same. Sharing love and compassion with everyone was how we would move forward, especially in the West, where the challenges were vast and our people ever-changing with newcomers from around the world. We didn't speak the same languages, but respect and love were universal.

I led her into the house and put her in a clean shirt. With my old horse, Jet, retired to pasture, I saddled up Ebony, the new black mare we'd bought, and headed out. I hoped the distraction would keep my mind from Sarah, at least for a little while.

Jackie enjoyed having Haiwee over, using each visit as a lesson in our language and customs. Haiwee had no shortage of teachers, and she seemed to soak up every new detail. With the two of them occupied, I rode to the saloon, my head full of questions. Would the tribe Lexi found be Haiwee's? If so, would Haiwee be headed home soon? Would she be safe with them? I adored the girl, but I knew it would be particularly hard on Sarah to let her go.

My breath held still for the briefest of moments as the thought settled in. Sarah had bonded quickly to Haiwee. No wonder she'd insisted on going to meet the tribe herself. Never mind the rest of the problems she faced, Sarah would want to meet Haiwee's family, see what they had to offer as far as care and safety if she were to return. Sarah would never trust that to anyone else, and it no doubt weighed heavy on her, adding to the mounting concerns Constance brought to the table.

Just when I thought I couldn't feel any worse about our argument, I had to go and have a moment of clarity.

I stepped through the swinging doors, barely managing a hello before Jade dropped everything, set her hands on her hips, and gave me that knowing glare of accusation. She'd had plenty of experience dealing with the aftermath of a Jo and Sarah fight over the years, and I prepared myself for the interrogation.

"What did you do?"

"Why's it always my fault?" Her response came in the form of a deepening scowl. "Fine," I spat, tossing up my hands in surrender. "But I did apologize, only she didn't fully accept. And you know what, Jade? I have to say that for being my best friend, you sure take Sarah's side a lot."

She chuckled and went back to wiping down the table. "Because I know you both and considerin' who she is and what she's capable of, you do tend to mother her a lot."

"I do not." My arms folded across my chest defensively, squeezing tight like a boa constrictor.

She laughed again as she moved on to the next table. "Why is this so sticky?" she grumbled, then stopped and focused on me once again, softer this time. "She didn't survive all those years without skills. She's smart and ferocious and deadly as hell when provoked. I know times are scary, and we worry for those we care about, but she'll come back." Jade eased into a smile. "There's no keepin' her from you, Jo."

The thump of my heart stuttered at her last words. It was true. Sarah had unbelievable tenacity, especially when it came to her love for me.

"Thanks, Jade."

"Anytime. Now, you gonna help, or just mope around?"

Through a laugh, I said, "Just a minute."

I walked out the swinging doors, greeting a young couple as they entered, then stared off at the horizon. The only way to truly calm the storm within would be talking to Sarah. For that, I'd have to be patient—not one of my best attributes. Not when it came to Sarah and definitely not when every hour felt like a hundred as the sun crept across the sky.

"Please come home safe, Sarah."

# CHAPTER TWENTY-FIVE

After dark, Sarah finally made it home. The clap of Clover's hooves against the hard ground put a smile on Haiwee's face every bit as wide as my own. Like oxygen had finally made its way into my lungs after too many minutes underwater, I gasped in a deep breath and peeked out the window. Hours had now dwindled to minutes, and with excitement also came nervousness that set the slightest tremor into my steady hands.

Would she be wounded? What mood would she be in? Did she get what she needed?

Haiwee sat on the floor, oblivious to my whirling thoughts as she played with her doll and a toy horse that resembled Clover. Rather than waiting by the window like a mountain lion ready to pounce, I took a seat beside Haiwee. As she offered me the doll to play along, the front door creaked open. From under the brim of her hat, Sarah's gaze locked on mine. Her jaw clenched. A hint of steel swirled in her expression, lying in wait for the moment it would rise to the surface and defend herself.

"Sawrah!" Haiwee squealed in joy as she grabbed the toy horse and ran toward her.

A smile forced a bend in her metal, and Sarah swooped the little girl up in her arms. They spoke in hushed tones, a seemingly serious conversation until Sarah stroked the horse's muzzle, then bopped Haiwee on the nose. Haiwee giggled and struggled to get down. After setting her safely on the floor, Sarah's eyes moved back to me, catching me smiling at their intimate interaction.

What kind of welcome would I get?

"Hey," I greeted in my most soothing tone. "Glad you're home." I stood and approached with tentative steps.

"Good to be home," she answered with a heavy sigh that uncoiled her shoulders. She removed her hat, set it on the peg by the door, and kicked off her boots. Last to go was her holster, which she walked to the bedroom.

My heart unclenched in relief. Haiwee had returned to her previous spot, playing happily with her toys, so I followed Sarah and pulled the door halfway shut. She removed her shirt and poured some water into the basin. I sat on the edge of the bed watching in the mirror as she washed up, thankful for the lack of fresh wounds. Once or twice, she caught my stare, and though she fought hard, that bashful grin made an appearance.

"I missed you," I admitted, not that it was any secret.

"I missed you too, Jo. Always."

"Even when I'm a horse's ass?"

A laugh blurted out, and she nodded. "Especially then," she said, turning around as she toweled off. "But you weren't an ass. You were concerned, rightfully so—"

"But I should respect your judgement by now because I trust you."

"I know."

"And I shouldn't put more stress on your shoulders when you're already carryin' so much weight."

"I can handle it."

"Doesn't mean you should have to."

"Look, Jo," her words breathed out with an exhausted sigh. "We know one another well enough to know you're gonna be overprotective and angry, and I'm gonna be hardheaded and storm off. But we love each other like crazy, and we'll come back to one another." Her eyes met mine, soft and full of love.

Wow! What to say to that?

Sarah slipped a sleep shirt over her head and removed her pants. I stood there in stunned silence, wondering when she had figured us out and why I'd been left out of the loop. She gave me that dreamy Sarah Sawyer smile as her fingers threaded into mine and pulled me close.

"You frustrate the Hell outta me, Jo Porter, but I love you." With the most tender of touches, she traced a finger along my jaw, staring at me with such reverence I could almost cry. "You're like water to my cactus."

"You are definitely prickly like a cactus," I lightened with a soft laugh. "But they don't need much water, my dear," I corrected, challenging her value of my worth with an arching brow.

Sarah rolled her eyes and laughed at herself. "Sorry, bad example."

"I hope so, but I know what you mean. You're the air that I breathe, Sarah." I returned her loving gesture, cupping her jaw in my palm and caressing the soft skin with a brush of my thumb.

"I like that one."

"Good. And here I was prepared to deliver a long drawn out apology."

"Honestly, I was ready to hash it out some more, but then I saw the two of you and none of it mattered."

Her confession sucked the air from my chest and filled it with something far more life-giving. I could never, would never, stop loving her. I pressed a tender kiss to her lips and rested my forehead to hers for a quiet moment.

"How did it go?" I finally asked, needing the rest of the answers to a day full of questions.

"Good. No trouble. They were surprised we wanted to help, but appreciative."

"And Haiwee?" My breath shuddered in wait of her answer. Glassy eyes said it all, and I let the air escape in a shaky exhale.

"She's theirs." Sarah swallowed down the lump in her throat, then added, "When this is over, if they survive, we'll take her back to her family."

I pulled Sarah into my arms. All I could do was hold her tight. She rested her chin on my shoulder and I threaded my fingers through her hair. "It's good she can get her family back," I soothed, pressing a kiss to her temple.

"Yeah," she breathed out. Sarah pulled back just enough to give me a quick kiss on the lips, then she continued, "I sent a telegram to the other sheriffs. Told them gather everyone they could and meet us here day after next at sunrise to go meet the tribe. Word is Constance is ready to move on them again."

"You do know I'm goin' with you, right?" It wasn't really a question.

"And you do know I'd prefer you stayed home, right?" she countered, matching my look of sheer determination.

Replaying her earlier statement regarding our heated interactions, I tried a new tactic. "So, does this mean we can skip all the back and forth and agree we're gonna ride into this together?"

She mulled it over a long moment, then shrugged. A hint of a smile buckled her armor. "Whether we like it or not, yes."

I could only laugh at the civility of discussing riding to our deaths together. Her smile stretched wide as the Idaho horizon, shoulders shaking with restrained laughter.

"Look at us," she said. "Jade would be proud."

"She would."

"But seriously, Jo. I don't want to argue, and I know you're not gonna listen on this one anyway, especially when other folks are joining in. So yes, together, for better or worse."

"Till death do us part?"

She shook her head and looked away. "Let's hope that's not yet," she said, turning back to me, smile absent, expression solemn.

"Agreed."

Her stomach grumbled. "I'm starvin'."

"You're in luck. I saved you some lamb."

"You're the best."

"I know." I let my embrace fall away, one hand still tethered to hers to lead her to the table.

She ate with her usual fervor. When she'd gotten her fill, Sarah graced us with a rare appearance of her guitar. She strummed a few chords to tune the instrument, drawing Haiwee's interest. As she began to play, the melodic tones of her hum drew Haiwee like a bee to a flower. She plopped down at Sarah's feet and gazed up at her in awe. Couldn't blame her. Sarah had a lovely voice, and I made a note to ask her to sing more often.

A few songs in, Haiwee added some of her own flair. She jumped to her feet and began to dance, stomping and singing something rooted deep in her culture I wish I understood—so beautiful, soulful. The moment brought one of the most heartfelt smiles out of Sarah I had ever seen.

Sarah caught my eyes, and in that moment, I knew we would be okay. I didn't know how, but determination burned bright through her joy and made it undeniable. Sarah Sawyer was a force of nature in her own right, and this time she would have an army on her side.

Once Haiwee had settled in for the night—she had finally gotten comfortable in her own bed—Sarah and I turned in as well. A full day of worry had exhausted me more than a full day of harvesting. I rolled to face her, and Sarah curled up close, our noses nearly touching. For a moment, we lay there, breathing one another in. She reached up, traced a lazy finger across my brow, then down the angle of my cheek, a smile curling her lips.

"You're so beautiful, Jo. I'm so lucky your heart chose me," she said with an air of awe. I could tell she was committing the moment to memory, the same as me.

"You are lucky," I teased with a laugh. "And it most definitely beats for only you." I pressed forward to give her a kiss.

She gathered me more fully into her arms until our legs intertwined, and my head tucked under her chin. The subtle smell of horses, sweat, and the musk so inherently Sarah filled my senses and brought about a sigh of joy. We were one another's rock. Despite our shared weakness of each wanting to keep the other safe, we would always be more formidable together.

"So...we're actually doin' this, huh? Takin' on the government?" We had to be crazy.

She tensed for a second, then relaxed with a long breath. "Yep," she said, pressing a kiss to my head. "And we're doin' it together."

"That's all I ever want. Let's give 'em Hell."

# CHAPTER TWENTY-SIX

**Sarah**

Unlike the previous times the tribe had been confronted by Constance's army of hired hands, the women and children were safely hidden and could not be used as leverage to persuade a quiet removal from their grounds. I understood all too well the power of having your loved ones used as a pawn, and I was thankful they wouldn't have to worry this time. Little things like that made a world of difference in a fight.

I, on the other hand, still had a stubborn Jo by my side, who I'd spend every second worrying about. With Jo's refusal to stay home—as if I had expected anything else from her—we left George in care of the farm and Clover. We had papers drawn up that he and his family would own our portion of the farm if anything were to happen to us. Jade would get full ownership of the saloon. Thankfully, we had talked both Jade and Nick out of coming. They had a son to raise now.

When I said my goodbyes to Clover, she sensed my uneasiness and seemed put out to be left at home. I already had Jo to worry about. I refused to put my best friend in harm's way as well. Clover would be in good hands with George. It took a load off of me to know she'd be well cared for and had her green pastures to enjoy.

Besides leaving Clover, the hardest part had been leaving Haiwee. We parted with a long held hug and suppressed tears, knowing she might never see us, or her own people, again. Death was surely a concern, but most of all, I didn't want to fail her. At least she would be safe with Kimama.

Jo and I had taken care of all the details in a way that unsettled me like no other battle before. I wasn't one for planning to die, even in times I'd been certain death stood waiting on my doorstep, but it was different with other people to consider and livelihoods at stake. Then, there was Edward. We held him up in the hills out of harm's way but near enough to witness and report on the outcome. An illustrator accompanied him along with a photographer. He had already sent a version of his story to Boise in case an ill fate should also befall him, but they were in wait of the true story. Soon, the ending would be revealed.

Shoulder to shoulder we stood, Jo to my left, the Chief to my right, and a little over a hundred others from three towns stretching either direction. The Indians decked out in war paint and full battle regalia mixed with men and women of all races who'd felt strongly enough about the cause to put their lives on the line. Jessie, Sam, Lexi, Charlie, Cody, Abe,

Mr. and Mrs. Jones, the Chen family, Sheriff's Herndon and Rawls, and many more. Faces I recognized and some I didn't, all armed with whatever they could find.

No one had any illusions of grandeur. We knew our chances were slim. Their numbers, skill, and weapons of choice were a mystery. All we had to go on was the tribe's last encounter, but would this attack be the same? Would we be formidable against them?

Not a clue, but here we were. Some on horses and some stationed to flank the area and create a crossfire. Others prepared with ropes, lassos, and plans to bring their horsed army to the ground for a more even fight. I was content to be on foot where I could take cover behind the many rocky mounds in the area. We were determined, and we would stand or fall together.

The wait dragged on, the sun moving slow the way molasses dripped from a cup. The heat of late summer bore down on us. Thank goodness for the brief reprieve offered by small gusts of wind, even if it brought with it the sting of dust against our reddened skin. Knot after knot twisted my stomach until I was sure it could never hold food again. The longer the wait, the paler everyone looked. Except for the stoic Chief. He had long ago perched himself on a large rock, staring into the distance.

Finally, as the day turned to dusk, the rumble of hooves carried through the air, closing in until the ground shook from the force that felt like thousands would appear. Once the dust had settled and our opposition lined across the horizon in a tight line, the realization of how unmatched we were, number-wise sunk in. I was certain we were also on the short end of experience and guns.

"What now?" Jo asked, catching me with a side glance. It was tiny, but I caught the tremble in her words.

"Not sure." I looked at Jessie, but she offered no help.

"We wait," said the Chief.

So we did. Constance and her crew probably hadn't anticipated the number of people who'd joined our cause. Or maybe they were as unsure of how to proceed as we were. Maybe having to face their own kind changed things. Suddenly, their job was no longer doing the West "a favor" by ridding it of the savages. There would be faces just like theirs looking them in the eye during the fight. Of course, they could be the type who cared little for life of any kind, and that would be bad news for us. Regardless, the battle was a lose-lose situation, one I hoped could still find a peaceful resolution.

When a trio of horses broke away from their line and headed toward us, I looked to Jo and Jessie, then to the Chief. He nodded, and the four of us began the ominous trek toward them. With each step that carried me closer to Constance, my nerves ebbed away, leaving only anger and disgust. The itch in my fingers returned, begging for action. We met twenty-yards out, face to face with the hired hands of those unwilling to bloody their own.

Did the lack of details help the men in charge sleep any better at night? Did the privilege of the ignorance of how their vile orders were carried out make it easier to go about their day?

*Repulsive.*

Adorned in dark blue from their hats to their boots, awaiting their orders in formation, Constance's men appeared every bit the well-trained army. Constance stood out from them all, not just because she was the only woman. Her red pussy-cat bow, and the shiny metal pin fixed to her vest, set her apart from the subdued sea of navy blue.

"Well, well, well. I might get to kill you after all, Sarah," Constance drawled with a cocky grin and a glint in her eye. The guys on either side laughed, one of them the man with the appaloosa.

"Funny, I was thinkin' the same about you."

"We can do this peacefully. We just need to push them into Montana, and we can be done here."

"Forgive me for havin' my doubts, given the murderin' and all, but that's not the land they were promised in the treaty. And what happens then? Another group pushes them further until they have no room to survive?"

Sensing the tension, anxious horses pawed at the ground and huffed, ready to lunge into action. Constance looked past us at the line of people set to defend the Indians. Her lips thinned into a tightly pressed frown.

"Why'd you have to go and drag all those people into this?" she asked, ignoring my question. "You can't stop it. You're only making the mess bigger for me to clean up."

"That's good enough reason alone." I let a small grin tug at my lips. "But I didn't drag them. They came willingly because they believe what's happenin' here is wrong and needs to stop."

"The writer was a nice touch, I'll give you that. But public sentiment is fickle. Once you're gone and no one hears of it again, all of this," she swirled her index finger around, noting our situation, "will fade away. It would all have been for nothing. Is that really how you want to die, Sarah?"

Constance turned her attention to the Chief, glaring at him for a long moment as if he would cower and withdraw. Instead, he stood tall, strong, and proud as he moved closer to my side. Constance slid her eyes to Jo, dragging her gaze up and down in a way that made me want to punch her out—or anyone else who looked at my Jo that way.

"You're ready to die for this too?" Constance asked Jo. "And you, Marshal? Seems a silly thing to do after retiring."

Jo answered the same as the Chief. She stood taller and pressed against my shoulder. Jessie did the same, her shoulder meeting Jo's in a sign of unity.

Head shaking in disbelief, Constance let out a huff of amusement, then said, "Love truly is a ridiculous thing." Her men laughed. "I fear you've read too much of that Shakespeare. Thouest lovers shall die together in an ill thought notion of savior," she spouted, quite proud of the terrible imitation that revealed a hint of her high-class, big city roots. "Who knew I was a romantic," she mused with a smirk. "I'd ask that writer to quote me, but alas, he too shall perish."

"You could do one of them plays in the big city," the man to her right proudly interjected, as if he'd ever even been to one.

"Pfft. She's got a long way to go," Jo said, erasing Constance's grin.

"This is the strangest discussion before a gunfight I've ever heard of," Jessie grumbled. "If talkin' bout Shakes-er-somethin' or other is what the world is comin' to, I'm okay with dyin' now."

"Enough of this," Constance growled, eyes fiery. "I've got a job to do."

"So do we," I said, matching her ferocity with my own. I stared her down, then we turned and started walking back to our line.

The Chief leaned in and asked, "Who is this man she speak of?"

I laughed at the sliver of light in the darkness. "A storyteller from England. It was a long time ago. Hard to understand the language really, but he seemed to like makin' his characters die in the name of love."

After a moment of thought, he said, "There is no more noble cause."

I walked the rest of the way in silence, weighing his words. He was right. Whether love of family or justice or belief, it was a powerful emotion to hang your hat on. I'd already lived it twice before.

Jo's hand slid into mine. When I glanced at her, she gave me a weary smile. Would these be our final few moments together? I had planned for many more nights of holding Jo by the fire under the night sky. More rides with Clover. More talks with Jessie.

A moment of doubt crept in—a terrible sign before a fight. I almost considered praying, but why change now? I'd gotten this far without it.

I slid my free hand down to trace along the edge of the pearl-handled revolver lying in wait. From the looks of the others, their thoughts echoed mine. Fingers and boots anxiously shuffled, the nervous energy causing them to shift their weight. Mouths in hard lines. Eyes wide in fear and anticipation as the seconds to confrontation ticked down.

Charlie stepped in and whispered, "It's not too late to back down, Sarah."

As if the winds had carried his words to every set of ears, all eyes landed on me. A large part of me wanted to, but I wouldn't be able to sleep at night with that knife of guilt twisting in my stomach. From the look in his eye, didn't seem like he could either. He'd come a long way from the man who hadn't wanted the responsibility of the badge a few weeks ago.

I shook my head. "For me, it is, but do what you need to do."

He nodded and moved back to his place, gripping his rifle tighter. Jo leaned in, whispering an "I love you" and pressing a gentle kiss to my ear that somehow managed to make my knees wobble and empower me to tackle giants at the same time.

"I love you too," I said, and for what I hoped wouldn't be the last time, I kissed her warm, soft lips. She smiled when I pulled away and my courage was restored.

I took two steps forward and addressed our army. "As I've warned before, this could get bloody. Anyone havin' second thoughts, now's the time to get. No one will think ill of ya."

For a long moment, no one moved, until a single body ran for the hills. Then, a second. But no more. Everyone else stood firm, and I couldn't help the swell of pride that all these people had chosen to stand up for the cause. I looked at Jessie. She settled her hands atop her guns, that familiar steel glinting in her eyes.

"I'm always with you," she said.

"All right then. We hold and let them make the first move." When she agreed, I checked with the Chief, who also approved. I called out the orders to the others, "They may try to herd us, but stay spread out. Circle around if needed, and keep cover when you can. We don't shoot unless they do. Got it?"

A chorus of acknowledgement rang out. The Chief relayed the order to his tribe and they readied themselves for battle. I hoped to keep the loss of life at a minimum on both sides. Constance, on the other hand...

When I returned to my spot in line, Constance's men had begun a slow approach. No turning back now. Those on horseback held the line as the rest of us spread out, set the ropes, and laid low. Neither side seemed excited to engage the other. Constance's army moved cautiously into our space. Our men on horseback refused to budge, resulting in shouting and pushing. When a few galloped past to break our line, up went the ropes, tripping their horses and bringing them to the ground.

Then, all Hell broke loose.

# CHAPTER TWENTY-SEVEN

Shouts and gunfire filled the air. When bodies began to fall, rage spurred me into action. My focus turned to Constance, who had lingered near the back, content to watch the melee unfold from a distance. She was a coward and an opportunist. Both made me sick to my stomach. I pressed my hand to Jo's back and pushed her in the direction I wanted to move. Engrossed in the battle, Constance didn't notice us circling. Her position near the rocks gave me the perfect spot to knock her from her high and mighty perch.

I scaled the boulder, Jo pleading with me to be careful as I ascended. When I reached the top, I peeked over the side. The Doctor salivated at the chance to pounce. It was almost too easy, but I couldn't talk myself into second guessing. I leapt off the side and wrapped my arms around her, sending us both to the ground hard and awkward. Groans of anguish filled my ears.

Were they hers or mine? Didn't know. Didn't care.

Anger drove my need to get to Constance. I shook the spots from my vision and rolled on my side. Pain pierced through my right shoulder, giving me pause getting to my feet. Good thing I could shoot with both hands. I could still make her bleed.

Jo rushed to my side and helped me up. Constance remained on the ground. She spat sand from her mouth and wiped blood from her chin. When she finally looked up, she stared right into my barrel pointed square at her face.

Time to pay her dues.

"Sarah," Jo cautioned.

Constance only smiled. "Killing me won't change anything. I don't make the calls."

"Then I'll consider it cleanin' up the filth." I leaned closer and pressed the barrel into her cheek. Her tender skin gave way to the force of my metal, and she flinched away in discomfort.

"Sarah, don't."

Usually, the soft touch of Jo's hand would return me to my senses, but knowing Constance had sent men to hurt Jo, only made me press harder. My finger twitched against the trigger with a mind of its own, desperate for the signal to squeeze and rid the world of one more person who only ever brought pain and anguish to others.

"Just do it, if that's what you're going to do." She talked tough, but the fear in her eyes betrayed all words. I loved having that power over her.

The urge was strong, oh so strong. Not since Myles, had I felt such a desire for blood.

"Sarah."

This time Jessie spoke up. I didn't acknowledge her either. I knew her angle.

"She needs to go to jail. Let justice be carried out lawfully."

A laugh rumbled up from my chest at the notion. Who was she kidding? "You know how that'll end. She's got powerful friends."

"That's right," Constance taunted with a smirk. "Guess it's up to you, Doc."

Was that a dare? She'd be a fool to think I wouldn't kill her. Maybe she thought I'd regret it, but I sure as hell hadn't regretted the others. Her death would be no different, even in an act of defiance against Jo's wishes.

"You're right," I said, the deadly tone of my words hitting the right chord as her smile faded.

"When you took that badge," Jessie said, butting in again, "you swore to uphold the law as Sarah Sawyer. Not to play judge and jury as the Doctor."

Something deep and angry rumbled within, a growl of resistance to my succumbing to better judgement. Despite the Doctor's protests, Jessie's sobering words pulled the red from my vision and my finger from the trigger. Jo's hand gave a gentle squeeze to my shoulder, and I blinked away my rage.

Constance took the opportunity to swat the barrel away. She rolled to her side and made to escape, but Jo's boot laid a quick path to her head, sparing no mercy in its force. Constance fell face down in the dirt with a groan of anguish. Jo pulled a piece of rope from her pocket and tied

Constance's hands behind her back. She gave her hostage a little extra shove into the dirt as she stood back up and gave Jessie a nod of thanks.

"I'll handle her," Jo said, her hand taking my free one and pulling it to her lips for a kiss. She leaned in and whispered, "It'll be okay. Go help the others."

She pulled away, that soft, comforting smile I loved playing at her lips—not at all fitting the war going on around us. I wanted nothing more than to escape all this craziness with her, to clear my mind and regain my balance, but work still needed to be done. My eyes drifted shut as I nodded. I drew in a long, deep breath and struck a balance between the dueling personalities of the Sheriff and the Doctor. With Constance handled, a singular goal returned to my mind—preserve as many lives as possible.

Jessie drew her gun, and we rushed back into the battle. Our older warriors worried me most. I spotted Mr. and Mrs. Jones, thus far unharmed and holding their own from a distance with rifles. Most everyone had been unhorsed, leaving dozens of bodies locked in skirmishes. The battlefield, vast and chaotic, was like nothing I had ever seen.

Where to even start? More important, how to get it to stop?

Movement caught the corner of my eye, and I spun around. A lone man in blue ran away from the fight. He stumbled, but hurried to his feet and kept moving as fast as he could.

"Maybe, if we hold out long enough, more will decide it's not worth dyin' over," Jessie said.

"I doubt we have enough time to wait that out," I said, skepticism heavy in my reply.

"We're holdin' up well."

I shook my head. What had I done?

"I shouldn't have let them do this." Never before had I been incapacitated by self-doubt, but there I stood, still as livestock in a storm. Putting my own life on the line was one thing, but watching everyone who'd come here because of my own desire to raise a fight...?

Another one fell to a knee.

Everything felt wrong.

A bullet struck a nearby rock, breaking me from my daze. We ducked for cover.

"They believe in the cause. They believe in you," Jessie said, firing a shot back. "Stop thinkin'."

At Jessie's prodding, a sudden flood of urgency pushed to the forefront. *Save as many as possible* chanted on repeat in my head, and I sprung back into action.

Off to my left, one of our own engaged in a battle. An attacker snuck up from behind, a stone raised high above his head with the intent of bringing it down on him. Firing off a quick shot, I hit him in the shoulder. The stone fell from his hands as he keeled over in pain. Jessie and I ran toward them, ready to dive into the frenzy, when shrill screams called out from our right.

Four riders with colors flying galloped at full speed toward us. One raised a trumpet to his lips and sounded the horn. All fighting stopped as everyone turned their attention to them. They brought their horses to a sliding stop a few feet from us, and I caught a clean look at the soldiers— U.S. Army cavalry. The lead soldier reached into his pocket and withdrew an envelope. He slowly opened it and unfolded the paper he'd pulled from inside. Green eyes stared at us before falling to the written words in hand.

"By decree of the President of the United States of America," his booming voice announced. "Any and all aggression towards the Indian Nation shall cease and desist immediately. The tribes shall be returned to their designated lands unhindered. Anyone who opposes or ignores this decree shall be persecuted to the full extent of the law. We have been instructed to escort them home."

When the words sunk in that we'd won, I nearly crumbled in relief. I rested my hands on wobbly knees and let the shock and awe of it all escape in a ragged breath. Jessie draped an arm over my back and let out a half sob. Her weight fell heavy on me as we held a silent moment of gratitude.

"You did it," she said, her voice thick with emotion in a way I'd never heard before. She tugged me into her and repeated, "You did it, Sarah."

I stood back up and wiped the sting of tears from my eyes with the back of my sleeve. "We did it."

"Sarah!"

Jo sprinted toward me, nearly losing her balance several times over in her haste. She jumped into my arms and delivered a bruising kiss. The salty trail of tears staining her cheeks spilled onto mine. She was safe and in my arms, and I needed to never do anything like this again. I held her close, soaked in the warmth and love that settled my soul. When I set her down, I felt more like myself than I had in weeks. Not even the pain in my shoulder could dampen my spirits.

Jessie gave me a proud nod as she and Jo embraced. Relief appeared to be the overwhelming emotion for both friend and foe. Constance's men collected their things and led their horses away. She wouldn't be going with them. Nope, she wouldn't be going anywhere except to jail for setting up those murders, slandering the good names of the Indian Nation, and sending men after Jo.

We made our way through everyone, shaking their hands, thanking them for their courage, and tending to their wounds. I found it remarkable that only a few had met their end on the battlefield as if neither side had truly wanted to harm the other. Standing in the remnants of the battle, watching everyone help one another regardless of skin, well, perhaps hope hadn't been lost for us yet.

The Chief, bloody but relatively unharmed, stood mourning over one of his own. Cody checked on Max, who had his arm held tight to his body. Charlie had bloodstains on his pants as he limped along. Mr. and Mrs. Jones packed up as if it were any other day in the field. Made me wonder what they used to get up to in their younger years.

Sam waved me over to old Abe, who lay motionless with a wound to his head. I knelt down and pressed my fingers to his neck—no pulse. I removed my hat and paid my respects. He had outlived his wife and kids, but rather than hide away and bide his time on his farm, he chose to stand up for what he believed in. That had been a life worth living.

"Sam, can I have your badge, please? I'll get you another one at home."

His brows crinkled at first, almost putout, until my reasoning dawned on him. He removed the star and handed it over. Eyes watering, he gave me a short nod. I slipped the pin through the worn fabric of Abe's white shirt and closed the back.

"Looks good on ya, Abe," I whispered, choking back emotions of my own. I stood up. "For your unwavering dedication to justice, I hereby deputize Abe Carson. It's been a pleasure to know you and fight by your side. May you rest in peace."

Sam etched the sign of the cross over Abe's head and said a short prayer. "I'll make sure he gets home safe, Sarah," he said, proudly taking responsibility for our fallen friend. The kid sure had grown up quick.

We began collecting the bodies and helping the wounded as we waited for the wagons to be brought up. The Chief approached, two warriors by his side. He clasped his hand to my elbow in a sign of friendship.

"You can go home now," I said, and his brown eyes warmed.

"Thank you. E aisen ne tei," he said, then added, "Means, you are my friend."

"You're welcome, my friend." I slid my right hand into his, then covered it with my left. "I'll go with you to make sure you get back safe."

"No need. You go home. Rest." He looked to Jessie, then Jo, smiling wider. "Take care of each other. We will see you again soon."

"We will," Jo said, tugging on my elbow. Once the Chief had gone, she leaned into my side and draped an arm low around my back. "Let's get everyone home to their families."

"I'm pretty sure Jackie's gonna have me sleepin' in the barn for a while for this," Jessie grumbled, rubbing the back of her neck.

Jo laughed and gave her a sympathetic pat on the back.

"Maybe, but at least it ain't winter," I teased.

She didn't seem to think it too funny. When she got back home though, I suspected it would be the exact opposite. Jackie would get her feelings off her chest, pin her with a stern glare, then keep Jessie all to herself for the next few days.

"You should take at least the rest of the week off from the ranch," I suggested. She had earned as much time as she wanted. "Ain't nothin' pressin' right now, and George has been handlin' everything fine."

Lexi trotted up on her horse, a little dusty, but no worse for wear. She gave us a once-over, then said, "Everyone's about ready to go."

"Oh," Jo jumped in startled surprise. "I almost forgot about Constance. She's tied up around the corner."

"We could leave her," Lexi suggested with a smirk and a gleam that said she'd been half-serious.

Tempting, but even my darkest side didn't favor exacting that type of death. Besides, I had the law to uphold. The length of my pause had Jo giving me a disapproving look and Jessie raising a questioning brow.

"Sarah…" Jo warned.

"Relax, you know I wouldn't do that." Or at least, I hoped she knew. "We'll load her up in a wagon and take her to jail. I'm sure the people in charge of this mess will want a scapegoat."

"I can't wait to get this story to Boise," Edward said, beaming with pride as he appeared from out of nowhere. "Thank the heavens, it'll be a happy ending."

"You're tellin' me," Lexi drawled. "Can't believe we're still breathin'. I'll go get the prisoner, then let's get to makin' tracks. I'm ready to get home."

She rode away, and we made our way to our wagon. Jo took her spot on the front seat. I settled in beside her. Jessie untied Silver and climbed up on his back. She assumed her usual place by my side.

"You know, Sheriff," Jessie said with a slow drawl. "I'm ready for those days when we sit on the front porch and reminisce like the two old ladies."

"Me too, old friend. Me too."

Grateful to still have my family by my side, I snapped the reins and our old reliable wagon horses, Dodie and Rebel, started our trek back home. I missed the days of just being a rancher, of quiet nights with Jo, but also took pride in helping others and continuing what Carter had built. The troubles of late weren't the norm. While our town needed a strong anchor when it stormed, there would also be plenty of days of smooth sailing ahead. We would relax and celebrate our win for now, but in the coming days, I'd have to decide who Sarah Sawyer would be for the foreseeable future. Rancher or sheriff.

# CHAPTER TWENTY-EIGHT

The dust had barely settled after the President had called off the terrible acts against the Indians and vowed to create a new treaty to protect the tribes. Probably wouldn't last. They'd find other ways to get what they wanted. But for now, all was right again. Governor Moody proudly gloated his supposed involvement in the remedy, even so far as to come back here for a posed photo shaking my hand. He already had the article written for the papers: "Governor Moody Delivers on Promise to Sheriff Sawyer."

Pfft. Only because he realized early on that any stake in the deed would quickly become a public nightmare. As name after name had been revealed in the news, he'd been wise to get out, claiming he did so "as soon as I had opened his eyes to the serious and vile injustice being done." As much as I loathed to go along with it, Jo said it would be a show of good faith for me to agree. So I did.

After a whole day of washing, I still couldn't get the slimy feel of his palm off of my own. Jo still insisted it would be worthwhile someday. Only time would tell. Jo then did her part to help me forget all about

Moody by replacing the memory of his hand in mine with the wet, wanting flesh of her own under my fingertips. There wasn't much Jo couldn't help me forget.

I awoke the next morning under the weight of a heavy cloud of sorrow. Haiwee's final day was upon us. Returning her to her family was the right thing to do, though my heart ached terribly at the impending loss. Ever the insightful woman, Jo knowingly snuggled into my side, one arm wrapping across my chest and a leg over my own. She pressed a series of kisses under my ear and held me close. The dam that held back my emotions shuddered against the force of feelings for the little girl. I swallowed them down, but Jo didn't miss the quake that rumbled through my body.

"I'll miss her too," she whispered, then pressed a soft kiss to my cheek.

No other words were spoken until we unraveled ourselves and prepared for the day. Jo was the first to step out of the bedroom, perhaps knowing I would prefer a minute to myself. I sat on the edge of the bed, fully dressed, hat and holster in hand, and breathed deep to collect myself. The door creaked open, and somber brown eyes peeked inside. In a blink, Haiwee arrived at my side, staring up at me with affection and gratitude. How I wished she could understand my words, but none were needed.

She reached for me, and I lifted her onto my lap. Haiwee immediately wrapped her small arms around my neck and hugged me tight. I held her close, and this time, the dam cracked. A tear broke free and rolled down my cheek. She pulled back with a watery smile and followed the tear until it fell from my cheek. A tiny finger wiped away its trail. She climbed down from my lap, took my hand, and led me to the other room where Jo had breakfast in the works. Jo glanced over her shoulder and smiled. She nodded to the table where coffee, milk, and sliced fruit had been set out.

Memories of my youth came flooding in—of Mom making biscuits while Dad sat at the table with me on his lap. He'd drink his coffee and flip through his medical books, explaining random cases to me. Those memories kept me warm when the frigid reminder of their absence crept in. The power of their loss also served as continuous fuel for the fire inside and drove every decision I'd ever made since that day.

I helped Haiwee into her chair, then slid the milk and fruit her way. Jo smiled as she set three plates of eggs and bacon on the table. On her way to her seat, she gave my shoulder a squeeze. Her touch brought a smile to my face, even as the weight on my chest prevented a full breath. The little girl attacked her food like a bear after hibernation and made no apologies about it. She'd need a full belly for the long ride ahead. When everything had been cleaned up, we gathered our supplies and headed to the barn.

Clover trotted up with a whinny when she spotted us. Like everyone else, my girl had taken a fast liking to Haiwee. She craned her long neck over the fence and stretched to meet Haiwee's small hand with her nose. Haiwee giggled at the soft touch and huff of air blown across her face.

"Hi, Clo-ver." Haiwee had only picked up a few words but spoke them pretty well. She held on to the fence and stood on her tiptoes to press a kiss to Clover's searching, wriggling nose, then giggled again when Clover mussed her hair.

It was hard not to sit back and let the two of them play, but we had to get ready to ride. Though I set the saddle against my hip and grabbed Clover's bridle, I couldn't resist watching a bit longer. Jo moved in beside me, her arm sliding around my waist and her lips finding purchase against my temple. We stood in silence for a few long moments and soaked in the scene before us.

"I know I should be happy she's goin' home, but…" Jo trailed off. She laughed when Haiwee giggled at Clover licking her hand. Haiwee held up her toy horse, and Clover gave it a lick too.

"Yeah," I said, swallowing down the lump clogging my throat like thick mud, a single word all I could muster. Any more, my voice would surely crack just like my heart.

Jo's hand brushed up and down my back. Thankfully, she didn't say anything else. I forced as much of a smile as I could for her sake, then opened the gate latch and began to saddle Clover. Jo grabbed a bridle of her own and caught Ebony.

Once we were all set, I sucked in a deep breath, looked at Haiwee, and held out my hand. "Ready to go home, Haiwee?"

Her smile still bright with the joy only a horse could bring, Haiwee took my hand and let me lift her into the saddle. Her little legs swung back and forth against the leather.

"Ta-ank you, Sawrah."

"You're welcome," I said, then turned to check on Jo. She'd already mounted her horse. "Ready?"

"When you are," Jo answered, laughing at the happy little girl in the saddle. But then, what little girl didn't love a horse? Especially Clover. She was a charmer.

"All right then," I mumbled and climbed up into the saddle behind Haiwee. I handed her the reins as I nudged Clover forward. "Let's get you back to your family."

Three hours later, we arrived at the tribe's new makeshift camp. Tomorrow they would travel the rest of the way home. Hopefully, word would spread and anyone who had been separated would make their way back safely. Too much blood. Too much loss. And for what? Greed, plain and simple. Why couldn't the government have brokered a peaceful option, or better yet, respected the rights of the Indians to say no and work around their reservation?

Again, greed, ego. A vast gap lay between us and the Indians in what we deemed important. I understood the idea of progress but despised the actions of destroying everything to achieve it. Life had existed just fine without telephones and those new automobiles. Electricity though, I did enjoy that one. But to be honest, I preferred the sight of Jo under candlelight.

Chief Running Bear parted the folds of his teepee and stepped outside. His wife and son followed. Soon after, several other members of the tribe were at their side, all with glassy eyes and full hearts at having one of their own returned. Haiwee's shoulders shook as the relief of seeing her family escaped in a sharp sob. I placed my hand on her back and stroked soothing circles until she calmed.

"Sarah. Jo," he said, voice thick with emotion as he placed a fist over his heart. "Thank you for bringing back our little dove."

I tipped my hat, holding my words until I could steady my voice. Jo looked to be in much the same state. The Chief spoke soft words in his native tongue, and Haiwee nodded. It was time.

Jo and I slid from our saddles, then I reached up for Haiwee. Her arms locked around my neck as I pulled her down, but I couldn't set her on the ground just yet. I had to hold her close for one last moment.

Haiwee squeezed tighter and whispered, "Will miss you, Sawrah."

"I'll miss you too. Stay safe." After another hug, I set her down.

She ran to Jo, who swooped the little girl up into her arms. She whispered into Haiwee's ear, then set her back on her feet. An agonizing pause held time still before she walked away, toy horse in her hand. Jo moved to my side, her arm finding that familiar place along my back.

Half-way there, Haiwee turned and ran back to us. Jo's hold tightened. The strength I had mustered to remain stoic took a blow, and I nearly let the tears flow free.

Haiwee hugged us one more time, then hugged and kissed Clover before she ran to her family. When Haiwee reached the Chief, he knelt to greet her, and they exchanged whispered words. He lifted her into his arms and stood up.

"Haiwee say she hopes this not the last you meet."

"I hope not." Somehow I felt fate would bring us back together. I only hoped it wouldn't be in the form of tragedy. "You know where we are if you need us."

"May the spirits protect you always."

The Chief's words were followed by the tribe chanting in unison. Their meaning may have been unknown to us, but I felt their power. With one last wave from Haiwee, the tribe engulfed her in a warm welcome.

That was our cue to head home.

# CHAPTER TWENTY-NINE

"I'm glad that's all over," Jo said, ambling from the house to our wooden bench beside the fire pit.

I worked the kindling to get the flames to catch. "Me too. Hope the Indians will be left alone now and Haiwee will be safe."

"Mhm. You did good, Sheriff."

I glanced over my shoulder. Jo's gaze followed my every move, like always, but with such love and pride, it overflowed into her wide grin and spilled into my chest. Jo's approval meant everything, but accepting a compliment still came as a challenge to me. I never sought a pat on the back for my actions, even when it meant something deeper coming from Jo.

Words stopped up in the back of my throat. I responded with a nod of gratitude and turned back to my task.

"I mean it," Jo pressed. "You didn't have to take up that fight, but you did, and you inspired our town to follow. You are always surprising and always passionate about doing what's right."

I mulled over her words, then finally, I shrugged and said, "I don't know any other way to live."

"It wasn't a complaint, Sarah," Jo teased, lips twisting into a wry grin. "I wouldn't want you any other way, even if it sometimes scares the hell outta me. That's also why you make such a great sheriff."

The flames climbed higher and higher until I was satisfied with my work. I set the poker aside and took my seat on the bench beside Jo, my arm finding its favorite resting place along her waist. She leaned into me and rested her head on my shoulder. Jo's hand intertwined with my free one, pulling it to rest on her knee.

Silence filled the space between us until the question niggling my mind needed answering. "So, you'd be okay if I decided to keep the badge a while?"

"If that's what you want, then yes. I'll worry, but there's no one I trust more."

"Thank you."

"Carter would be proud," she said. Sadness weighted her praise.

I fought the thick lump threatening to close my throat to croak out, "I hope so."

Jo nuzzled into the crook of my neck. "I love you," she whispered.

Pressing a kiss to the top of her head, I spoke those words that meant everything to me. "I love you too, Jo."

I enjoyed the gift of a quiet moment with the woman who'd given me the life I never imagined, the life I would never trade for the world. Again, silence stretched on, long and comfortable. That trait sat near the top of the list of things I loved most about Jo, how we could just…be. And there we stayed until those roaring flames faded to embers.

My mind, my heart, were full of an infinite amount of thoughts and feelings I couldn't find words to describe. Maybe someday I would, but not today. Today, I didn't want to think or feel or sift through the meaning of why it felt like the end of something big and the beginning of something new and wonderful.

Jo's lips latching onto my neck made it easy to forget everything else in the world.

"What are your plans for tomorrow?" she asked in a soft whisper, careful not to disrupt the peaceful mood of the evening. Her thumb began a soothing back and forth across the back of my hand.

"I imagine much the same as any other day. Why?"

Jo stood up, keeping my hand in hers, facing me with a smile that called like a siren to a sailor. She took slow steps backward until our arms had reached the end of their lengths. "I know a way we can forget about life for a while."

My lips curled. "Do you now?" A slow nod her reply, she tugged me up and continued her backward stride. "Care to let me in on it?" I asked, my smile growing wider.

"I'll give you a hint. It's something you're really good at."

"That could be many things."

She rolled her eyes and laughed. "It's also something I really enjoy you doin'."

"Again, many things…"

"So proud of yourself, Sheriff."

I chuckled, following her as I always did and always would.

"How bout this one? It's something we're really, really good at together." When I hiked my brow, enjoying our little game, she added, "And it doesn't involve guns or knives."

At that, I pretended to think long and hard, but when she bit into her lower lip, eyes glinting from the moonlight, the time for games ended.

"I do seem to recall one thing."

Her eyes grew wide when I charged forward and scooped her up over my shoulder like a potato sack. A yelp echoed into the night as I rushed up the steps and into the house, kicking the door shut behind us. Shared laughter filled the room when Jo pretended to struggle, but when we reached the bedroom, and I dropped her onto the bed, the mood shifted.

One by one, I undid the buttons of my shirt. As if I were standing barefoot on a bed of coals, her fiery gaze heated me from my feet upward. Beads of sweat dappled my forehead. The momentary pause served as kindling. Flames wicked upward into a frenzy, engulfing us both. Clothes couldn't come off quick enough as Jo and I shed one another of the rest of our garments.

Finally skin to skin, arms and legs tangled, we both released sighs of relief and contentment that drew matching laughs. Jo bumped her nose against mine, then drew me in for a kiss that read like a prophecy of my future—hot, wet, passionate, and a whole lot of Jo. But I didn't need a prophet to tell me I'd be right here, in this woman's arms, loving and being loved until the end of our days.


**THE END**

# ABOUT THE AUTHOR

S.W. Andersen writes Sapphic romances where love knows no bounds. This is her seventh novel, including two best-sellers. Having been raised by her mother, a strong female character in her own right, she has always been attracted to stories that depict independent, capable, determined women. While life tends to surround us with negativity, she prefers to fill it with happily ever afters.

S.W. has spent a large part of her life around horses and rodeos, and has always had an affinity for the cowgirl lifestyle. Her love of the mountains and westerns were the driving forces behind her Sarah Sawyer western series. When she isn't working, she enjoys outdoors activities and traveling with her wife, Dianna. They share their ten acres in rural Florida with a rambunctious crew of dogs, cats, and horses.

CONNECT WITH SW:

swandersenwrites.com

# MORE BOOKS BY S.W. ANDERSEN

Cowgirl artwork by the very talented Rafi DeSousa

@RafiDeSousa

Rafidesousa.tumblr.com

www.ingramcontent.com/pod-product-compliance
Lightning Source LLC
Chambersburg PA
CBHW030257200626
46816CB00002BA/675